THE BILLIONAIRE'S COWBOY GROOM

A SWEET BILLIONAIRES ROMANCE

LORANA HOOPES

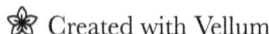

NOTE FROM THE AUTHOR

Thank you so much for picking up this book. After readers read The Billionaire's Christmas Miracle, I got a ton of emails wanting Drew and Gwen's wedding, so I obliged and decided to give Carrie her own story as well.

In addition, you'll see Max and Alyssa again from The Billionaire's Secret. If you haven't read it, be sure to pick it up to hear their story, and you'll get a glimpse of Sam and Brent from Brush with a Billionaire.

I hope you enjoy the story and the characters as they are dear to my heart. If you do, please leave a review at your retailer. It really does make a difference because it lets people make an informed decision about books.

Sign up for Lorana Hoopes's newsletter and get her book, The Billionaire's Impromptu Bet, as a welcome gift. Get Started Now!

Lorana's Other Billionaire Books:

The Billionaire's Secret

Brush With a Billionaire

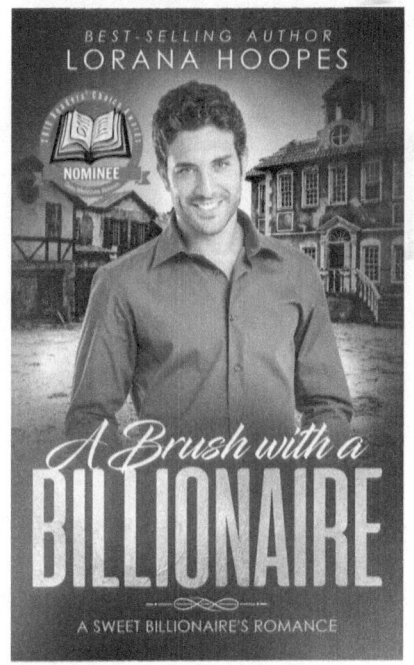

The Billionaire's Christmas Miracle

The Cowboy Billionaire - coming soon!

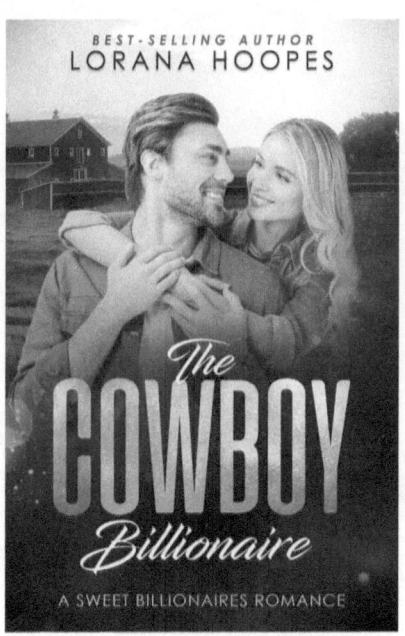

BEST-SELLING AUTHOR
LORANA HOOPES

The
COWBOY
Billionaire

A SWEET BILLIONAIRES ROMANCE

CHAPTER 1

*C*arrie zipped up the back of her best friend's dress and stepped back to admire it.

"Oh my goodness, Carrie, this is more beautiful than I even imagined." Gwen fingered the white satin, her hand trailing across the lace and bead detail. She turned and studied the image in the full-length mirror. With her red hair pulled up, her slender shoulders were even more defined in the strapless dress.

"Well, you deserve it. Besides, if you are going to marry Drew Devonshire and become a Devonshire, then you must dress like one." Carrie smiled at the vision that was Gwen. The white pearls and lace accentuated her creamy skin, and her green eyes sparkled. Happiness filled Carrie that she was able to make Gwen feel so good about herself.

"You are the best friend a girl could ask for." Gwen turned from the mirror and enveloped Carrie in a hug. "Now, let's get you dressed. Alyssa should be back soon."

Gwen had met Alyssa a few months after Drew proposed. Evidently, Drew had gone to college with Maxwell Banks, and they had reconnected when Drew searched for friends to make his groomsmen. It hadn't been too hard to find him considering they were both billionaires.

Max and Alyssa had visited, and Gwen and Alyssa had hit it off. They became close enough friends that Gwen had asked her to be a bridesmaid. Carrie didn't mind. Gwen needed more friends, and she liked Alyssa too. And of course, Peyton was a doll.

The door opened then and Alyssa and Peyton rushed in. Well, Peyton rushed in, Alyssa's entry was more of a waddle seeing as how she was eight and a half months pregnant. "Sorry, Gwen, when you gotta go, you gotta go."

"Wow, Miss Gwen, you look so pretty," Peyton stared up at Gwen with wide eyes. "Almost as pretty as Mommy looked when she married Daddy." Peyton looked back to Alyssa, her eyes full of admiration.

The girls all laughed. "Well, I wouldn't expect to look prettier than your mommy." Gwen smiled at Alyssa over Peyton's head. "And don't worry about the time. Your dress is here. Carrie was just about to get dressed as well."

"I realize it's not my wedding, but I feel like a chicken with its head cut off." Alyssa patted her pregnant belly. "How do you two keep up here?"

"I hire help." Carrie laughed as she slipped out of her clothes and into her bridesmaid dress. The emerald green satin hugged her figure like a second skin. She was glad she had been so strict with her diet lately, or the dress might not have fit her. "I've had to hire another designer to help me."

"It's because you are so amazing," Gwen said. "I mean this dress is stunning." She twirled in front of the mirror again.

"I'd say she's a fan." Alyssa chuckled as she stepped into her own emerald green dress. Gwen had chosen emerald green because she thought both Carrie and Alyssa would look good in it. Alyssa's hair was a dark brown unlike Carrie's red locks, but the emerald green was a color that brought out the best in both of them. "I wish I had known you when I got married. I would have loved to have worn a dress you designed."

Carrie stepped over to the mirror to check her reflection. "I saw your wedding picture. Your dress was beautiful."

"Did you see my dress at Mommy's wedding too?" Peyton asked. She was already in her flower girl dress and practicing throwing fake petals from her basket.

Carrie turned, smiled, and squatted down to the little

girl's level. "As a matter of fact, I did. You looked just as pretty then as you do now." She tapped the end of the girl's nose earning a giggle in reply.

"Yes, it was beautiful," Alyssa said picking up the original thread of conversation again, "but there's something about having a friend make your dress that makes it extra special. I mean if you hadn't made this one, I doubt I would have found one that fit. I am as big as a house."

"You're welcome and you still look radiant," Carrie said. "When is the baby due?"

"A month. Can you believe that? It's a good thing you didn't plan this wedding any later, Gwen or they might not have let me fly."

"I'm sure Max would have found a way to get you here," Carrie said with a laugh. "I don't know him well, but he seems like a take charge kind of guy."

"Oh, he is that all right." Alyssa smoothed her dress and turned in front of the mirror. "What about you, Carrie? When are you going to marry that handsome French man I met? What was his name?"

"Philippe." Carrie shrugged her shoulders. "I'm not sure. He hasn't asked yet, but we've only been dating a few months." Of course, that was forever in Carrie's dating history. For as long as memory served her, she had flitted from one man to the next. Obviously, she was looking for something, but she wasn't sure what yet. She hoped she it would smack her in the face when she found it so she didn't miss it.

"Well, I'm sure it will be beautiful whenever it happens." Alyssa rubbed her belly again.

"And I'm sure this baby will be beautiful," Gwen said. "You better send pictures."

"Of course I will. Chances are he'll resemble this one though." She hugged Peyton to her. "Max's genes seem to run strong. Thank you, Gwen, for letting her be your flower girl."

"Yes, thank you, Miss Gwen. I promise to do a good job." Peyton's innocent face held the sincerest expression Carrie had ever seen on a person so young.

"I know you will, sweetie. Your mom said you are a natural at throwing flowers. And I have no younger sisters or nieces, so you are doing me the big favor." Gwen picked up the bag of flower petals and filled Peyton's basket.

Suddenly music carried into the room. "I think that might be our cue," Carrie said. "Everybody ready?"

"I can't believe it's finally time." Gwen's voice dripped with happiness and awe. Her face shone, and her smile stretched from one ear to the other.

As Carrie opened the door and led the way to the sanctuary, she wondered if she would ever have the same expression on her face. When would it be her turn?

*C*al Roper looked down into the basket of baked goods as he tried to come up with the right words. Though everything looked and probably was delicious, he needed to find some way to make Ginny understand he wasn't interested in her romantically. She was as sweet as cherry pie, but he preferred apple.

"Thanks, Ginny, this was real nice of you," Cal said as he looked back up at the perky blond.

"Oh, you know me, Cal, always baking more than I need." She dropped her eyes to the ground and her toe dug a circle in the soft dirt. "So, I thought to myself - who could use some homemade goodies? And you popped right into my head." She glanced up and flashed him a megawatt smile revealing nearly every one of her teeth as she batted her eyes at him.

Cal supposed she was waiting for more than a thank-you. An invitation to dinner maybe or a ride on the mares, but he couldn't do it. He wouldn't lead the poor girl on.

"Well, I do appreciate it, and I'm sure Stacy will as well, right, sis?" He flashed his sister a help-me-out-will-you glance as he spoke.

Stacy opened her mouth to reply, but Ginny beat her to it. "Not that I'm sure you're not a good cook, Stacy," she added as if just realizing how insulting her words might have sounded to his sister.

Stacy held up her hands. "I take no offense. Cal does his own cooking. I just work here, but I'm sure we both will enjoy these muffins. It was real sweet of you to think of Cal."

Ginny smiled again and turned her eyes back to Cal. Her smile faltered when she realized he wasn't going to extend any sort of invitation. "All right, well I better be getting my own dinner going, so I guess I'll see you both at church on Sunday."

"We'll be there," Cal said, "and thanks again." He lifted the basket and forced a small smile.

"She likes you," Stacy said as Ginny walked away.

Cal sighed and dropped the basket onto the porch. "I suspected." Ginny was a nice girl. Cute with a bubbly personality and a believer, but his heart belonged to someone else.

"But?" Stacy pressed.

Cal shrugged. "But I'm not interested."

"You haven't been interested in the last three women who have shown an interest in you. You didn't have enough in common with Gabriella, you had too much in common with Heather, and Sophie lived too far away."

"Well, she did," Cal said. "I don't want a long-distance relationship."

Stacy fixed her steely gray eyes on him. She might be a year younger than him, but she could turn a heart to ice with her fierce expression. He would want her watching his back in a fight any day. "Cal, it's been six years. When are you going to let that woman go?"

"When God tells me it's time." He took his Stetson off and wiped the light sheen of sweat from his forehead though he wasn't sure if the sweat was from his recently finished chores or this conversation. "I know you think I'm crazy, but I married her and that means something to me. God hasn't told me it's time to move on yet, so I'm going to follow His will until He does."

Stacy's eyes softened. "Cal, I understand you want to do God's will, but you married this woman on a whim in Vegas. That's not what God had planned when He created marriage."

Cal nodded. While Stacy didn't have the whole story, she was right that he shouldn't have married the woman. Cal hadn't even believed in love at first sight, but when he'd seen the fiery red head in the casino, his heart had jumped. It spun. It danced the tango in his chest, and he just knew he couldn't lose her. After spending hours talking with her, he'd proposed to her, and she'd said yes. An all-night wedding chapel had been delighted to take their money, and Cal had spent an amazing night with the woman. Unfortunately, she hadn't been quite as excited about the marriage the next morning. She had begged him for an annulment and when he'd refused, she had thrown her ring at him and left.

"I know you write her every year." Stacy continued

breaking into his walk down memory lane. "Has she ever responded?"

"Not yet, but she will." Every year on their anniversary, Cal sent her a card requesting a rekindling of their relationship. Every year, he heard nothing from her - he honestly wasn't even sure if his letters were even getting to her. Still, Cal felt deep down in his bones that someday he would hear from her. He might not have waited on God's timing to marry her, but now that they were married, he was determined to wait on God's timing to make it right. And God kept telling him to wait. So, he would. He would wait as long as he had to.

C arrie linked arms with Scott as Alyssa and Max reached the front. She had hoped to be able to walk the aisle with Philippe, but Scott was Drew's best friend. It only made sense he would be the best man. Besides, she would have plenty of time with Philippe at the reception, and he would be sitting in the first few rows on Gwen's side. She would have a great view of him.

"Ready?" Scott asked.

"Absolutely." In step, they walked up the aisle parting ways at the stage. Carrie stepped to her left to stand beside Alyssa and Scott went to his right to stand between Max and Drew. Carrie turned to face the congregation as the music changed. Her eyes scanned for Philippe first who flashed her a charming smile. She returned it and then shifted her gaze to the back of the church to watch Gwen enter.

The lights hit the pearls and sequins on the dress as she entered, and Carrie smiled as gasps of delight echoed around the room. She had never been prouder of one of her designs.

Gwen handed her the bouquet as she stepped on the platform and took Drew's hands.

"Dearly beloved, we are gathered here today to celebrate the marriage of Gwen Rodgers and Drew Devonshire. On the outside, they may seem like opposites - a teacher and a billionaire - but they have learned one of the most important lessons in life. They have learned to see past money and outside appearance and into the heart. It's what's in the heart that matters most, and in that respect, they are two of a kind. They love each other, and they love the Lord."

Carrie glanced at Philippe as the minister spoke. "You look beautiful," Philippe mouthed to her, and a blush stole across her cheeks. Could he be the one for her? She hadn't seen any red flags that sent her running yet, but she had expected to feel something different if he was the one. Some tug on her heart, the sound of fireworks, something.

"Do you Drew, take this woman as your wife to have

and to hold through sickness and in health, forsaking all others until death do you part?"

Carrie shook her head to clear the thoughts. She had a job to do, and she needed to pay attention.

Drew's smile lit up his whole face as he said, "I do."

"And do you Gwen take this man as your husband to have and to hold through sickness and in health forsaking all others until death do you part?"

"I do."

"Then by the power vested to me by the great state of New York, I now pronounce you husband and wife. You may kiss the bride."

Carrie cheered along with the rest of the congregation as Drew leaned forward and kissed Gwen. Then they faced the church and held their hands up before running out the aisle. Carrie took Scott's arm and followed suit. They burst out the doors and joined Gwen and Drew in the foyer. Max, Alyssa, and Peyton joined them a moment later.

"Congratulations, Gwen," Carrie said enveloping her in another hug. "You looked so beautiful."

"I'll second that," Drew said. "Carrie, that dress is perfection."

"Well, I had a good model." She handed the bridal bouquet back to Gwen. "You might need these."

"I might, but I have a sneaking suspicion it'll be

finding its way back to you soon enough." Gwen took the flowers and flashed a knowing glance at Carrie.

"I'm not sure about that," Carrie said with a shake of her head. "Philippe doesn't seem in any hurry to propose."

"He will," Alyssa said joining the conversation. "I predict a wedding in your near future."

Carrie appreciated the sentiments of her friends, but she wasn't so sure. Philippe may have been her longest relationship in years, but they were only going on four months. It was way too early for him to propose, and she was still sorting out her feelings. "Come on, we better get to the reception area before the stampede hits," Carrie said changing the subject.

"Just not too fast." Alyssa placed her hands on her large belly. "This pregnant woman can only go so quickly."

"We'll see you there in a minute," Gwen said as Drew pulled her toward the holding room where they would wait a few minutes to give the rest of the congregation time to get to the reception area.

Carrie led the way down the hallway and opened the doors to the reception area. It was decorated with white lights and tulle. White roses nestled in green foliage covered every tabletop and large windows granted expansive views of the city. The elegance, though understated, permeated the room. Gwen's personality shone through in every simple touch.

"Wow," Peyton said beside Carrie. "It looks like a princess lives here."

Carrie nodded. "Her wedding planner was pretty amazing, but I think most of this was Gwen's idea. I'm guessing that's our table up there on the stage. Shall we go find a seat?"

"Yes, please," Alyssa said. "I would love to get out of these shoes."

By the time they sat down, the rest of the guests were making their way in. Philippe joined Carrie at the head table. "That was a nice ceremony."

"It was." Carrie stared at him a moment wondering if he ever imagined what their wedding might look like.

"Ladies and gentlemen." The DJ's voice interrupted her moment, "please welcome for the first time Mr. and Mrs. Devonshire."

The room erupted in clapping and cheers as Gwen and Drew walked over to their table. As soon as they sat down, the waiters began bringing out the dishes. Carrie only picked at the delicious food, afraid if she ate too much that she would bust the seams on her dress. It was already getting uncomfortable just from sitting.

When the bride and groom finished eating, Scott and Carrie each gave their toast, and then Gwen and Drew danced their first dance.

"Come on." Carrie grabbed Philippe's hand when other couples were invited to the floor. This was the moment she had waited for. Carrie loved dancing and Philippe would never indulge her, but surely, he wouldn't say no at a wedding. It was expected guests would dance at a wedding.

"I don't dance," he said with a shake of his head. "I've told you that before."

"I understand, but it's my best friend's wedding. I want to dance at her wedding."

"Two left feet." He pointed to the floor. "Don't like making a fool of myself."

"But what about our-" Carrie snapped her mouth shut. She had been about to ask him about their wedding and he hadn't even proposed yet. She must be caught up in the wedding fever.

"Our what?" he asked.

"Nothing, I'm going to grab some punch." She turned away before the hurt expression on her face displayed her true feelings. If they did marry, would he not dance with her? Surely, he would make an exception for his own wedding.

"May I have this dance?"

Carrie looked to her left to see Max staring at her with his hand outstretched. "No, it's fine, really."

"Come on, Alyssa sent me over here. She's too pregnant to dance. Besides, it might help your man see what he's missing."

Carrie glanced over at Alyssa who smiled and shot her

a thumb up sign. "Okay," she said with a laugh. "If it's all right with Alyssa. She's a pretty amazing woman."

Max situated her in his arms when they reached the dance floor. "Don't I know it. She's way too good for me. You know, I never expected I'd marry. I was rather like you - a serial dater, though I wasn't as nice about it. I was pretty awful to the women I dated." He spun her around. "My point is that if I can find love, you can too."

"Thank you." Carrie smiled up at him. He might not have started out a kind man, but he certainly was now.

After Max, she danced with Scott, then Drew, then random guests who came and asked her. It almost seemed as if they were keeping her busy to distract her from remembering her own date's refusal to dance, but Carrie didn't mind. Before she knew it, it was time for the bouquet toss. She lined up with the other women, and Gwen's aim was as true as her word. The bundle of flowers landed squarely in her hands.

"I told you," Gwen said before she was whisked away.

Carrie smiled and then turned to Philippe. She almost laughed at the pained expression on his face as she held up the bouquet. It was a silly tradition, but she couldn't help hoping that maybe catching the bouquet would turn things around for her. With all her friends married or getting married, she was starting to long for that solid foundation as well.

CHAPTER 2

"Carrie, you are not going to believe this." Excitement filled Gwen's voice as she burst through Carrie's boutique door.

Both Sierra's and Carrie's head shot up at the outburst. Carrie dropped the paper she was sketching on and rushed to her friend throwing her arms around her. "Gwen, you're back. I've missed you so much."

Gwen laughed as she returned the embrace. "It's only been two weeks, Carrie."

"I know, but I've been so bored without you here."

"Hey," Sierra piped up from the back of the store where she was working on an alteration. "What am I? Chopped liver?"

Carrie flashed an apologetic glance toward her assistant. "Sorry. I've just missed my best friend."

"Well, I doubt boredom will plague much longer. Did you see this?" Gwen held up the paper clasped in her hand.

Carrie took it and scanned the page. Her eyes widened as she read the headline. "The wealthy elite may have found their next Vera Wang in Carrie Bliss?" She sped through the rest of the article which highlighted Gwen's and Drew's wedding and included a large picture of Gwen's dress. Underneath it was an entire paragraph dedicated to Carrie and her business. She looked up at Gwen. "When did this run?"

"A few days ago. Are you telling me you really hadn't seen it?"

Carrie shook her head. She rarely read newspapers or even watched the news. "No, but my phone has been ringing off the hook with orders since yesterday. I guess this explains it. I'm going to need to hire another few seamstresses to help me sew all these dresses."

"Yes, please," Sierra's voice carried from the back.

"Carrie that's amazing. I bet you'll hit billionaire status before the end of the month."

Carrie hadn't even made that connection. It was what she wanted more than anything in the world, but she thought it would still be a few more years in the future. She'd only been a multi-millionaire for a few years. However, with Gwen's wedding dress splashed all over the page and her name listed as the designer, perhaps she would hit it sooner than she thought.

"We should celebrate," Carrie said. "Do you think Drew will let me pry you away from him for dinner tonight?"

Gwen smiled. "I'm sure he could use a break from me, but what about Philippe? How are things on that front?"

"Same as ever." Carrie shrugged. "I finally find a man I might want to commit to and he has no desire. Always the way, right?"

"I'm sure he'll get there. Sometimes, it takes men a little longer to realize what they have." Gwen squeezed her arm and offered a sympathetic smile.

"Yeah, you're probably right," Carrie said. The phone began ringing again behind her, and she sighed. "You know what? Let's start the celebration early."

"What about your orders?" Gwen asked indicating the ringing phone.

"Let Sierra get it. It's partly what I hired her for." In truth, she had hired Sierra to help her sew, but answering phones had been a small part of her job description. Today, it would just be a larger part. She would need to get more help started soon.

"Okay, if you're sure. I would love to catch up."

"And tell me all about the honeymoon." Carrie ducked behind the counter to grab her purse. "Sierra, I'm heading out for the day. Don't forget to lock up."

Sierra, phone to her ear, shot Carrie a look of frustration but waved. Carrie would have to do something nice for Sierra after leaving her with all the work today, but she so wanted to catch up with Gwen.

"Well, I'll tell you some of the honeymoon, but I'm keeping some parts to myself," Gwen teased as they exited Carrie's boutique.

*C*al sighed and raked a hand through his hair as he stared down at the bill. Even if he sold half his cattle, he would only buy himself a few months. He needed a miracle and he needed it soon.

"Not good news, huh?" Stacy's voice carried across the room and he turned to see her leaning in the doorway.

"No, it's not. That sickness last year hit us hard. We don't have nearly the herd we would have had this year if half of them hadn't been wiped out."

"So, what are you going to do?"

Cal let out his breath and shook his head. "I have no idea. I'll sell half of what I have, see if I can get an extension on the loan, and pray."

"Cal, I know you don't want to think about it, but Ginny's family is wealthy. Maybe if you-"

Cal cut her off before she finished. "I'm not doing it, Stacy. I will not court a woman just for her money.

Besides, I'm still married, and I'm not giving up on her yet."

Concern filled Stacy's eyes. Cal knew she worried about him. She was already married and had a wonderful family, and he… he was still waiting. Waiting for a woman who might never come around. But right now that was a good thing. He didn't need any added distractions while he thought about how to save his ranch.

"All right, Cal. Well, will you come to dinner? Annie and Trevor miss their uncle."

"I'll try, Stacy. I've got a lot to do today." He needed to check on the cattle and the fence to make sure there were no weak spots. Cal certainly couldn't afford to lose any more cattle. Then perhaps he would ride over to The Morrison ranch to see if the fellow rancher might be interested in a trade. If he could save on the price of hay, another month of payment might be possible. It wasn't much but it might give him time to come up with another plan.

The concern on Stacy's face deepened. "Don't work too hard, Cal. There's more to life than the ranch."

Maybe for her - she had the general store to fall back on - but Cal was born to ranch. He was happiest when he was on his horse with the sun shining down on him. Yes, he could probably find another job where he rode, but it wouldn't be the same. There was something about owning your own piece of land that he would miss if he was forced to sell it.

"I'll come by soon. I promise." He grabbed his hat off the desk and gave her a hug before continuing to the back door.

The warm air kissed his face. Cal scanned the horizon, but the sky was clear. There would be no rain today. With a sigh, Cal continued to the barn and saddled up his favorite horse, Ginger. Her coat was the color of chocolate - more brown than red, but he couldn't bring himself to name her Chocolate when he bought her six years ago, so he'd picked Ginger. She had been his first purchase when he took over the ranch, and he probably shouldn't have bought her. Buying her sent him upside down the first year, and he had yet to recover fully, but she was worth the cost as far as he was concerned.

"All right, girl, let's go for a little ride, shall we?" He walked her out of the barn and shut the door. Then with a graceful ease, he swung himself onto the saddle. The hard leather of the saddle didn't mold, not really, but he felt like it did. In the saddle was where he belonged and there was always a sense of coming home when he mounted up.

He led Ginger along the north side of the property first. The Morrison ranch was to the south, so he might as well save it for last. His eyes scanned the fence as he continued down the line. It appeared to be in decent shape, but it ought to - the snow the previous winter had buckled several pieces of wood and he'd had to replace a good portion of the fence. That had been another unseen expense especially as Soda Spurs didn't get snow that often.

Satisfied the fence was in good condition, he turned his attention to the herd. There were too many to count individually, but he had learned a long time ago to scan the herd and visually identify ten to twenty at a time. It wasn't a perfect count, but it was one he could do daily and be fairly accurate. He did a more thorough count once a week.

When he was confident no cattle were missing, he scanned the grass. It was looking a little thin on this side. He'd have to move the herd soon and hope for rain. If he could just catch a break, he might be able to start turning a little profit.

Cal urged Ginger toward the south fence. He'd worry about the grass tomorrow. Right now, he needed to finish checking the fence. The wood on this side also appeared in good shape, so he led Ginger off his property and over to Don Morrison's ranch.

Cal found Don working with a new colt in his corral. Frustration creased the older man's face, and a stiffness filled his posture.

"Hey, Don, you got a minute?" Cal asked as he pulled Ginger to a halt.

Don looked up and smiled. "Sure, Cal, I need a break

from this guy anyway." He led the colt back to the barn and Cal dismounted. A few minutes later, Don returned. "So, what can I do for you?"

"That illness last year hit my herd pretty hard. I was hoping perhaps you might be interested in a little trade to save money. I could break that colt for you if you have extra hay or grass."

Don rubbed his chin as he considered the offer. "This one is being more difficult than normal. I could save some time if I wasn't having to break him. All right, Cal, you got yourself a deal."

"Thank you, Don." The two men shook hands and exchanged small talk for a little longer before Cal bid him goodbye and returned to his ranch. It wasn't a permanent solution, but he would take all the time he could get.

CHAPTER 3

*C*arrie stared at the paper in her hand. Wow, that happened quickly. The story on Gwen's dress ran only a week ago, and while orders had quadrupled, Carrie hadn't expected her wealth to increase with such speed. Still, it pleased her. She felt... secure for the first time in a long time.

It was stupid really. She had always been wealthy; her father had been a millionaire. He even gave her a trust fund to get her shop started, but shortly after college, her father had been diagnosed with cancer. The resulting medical bills wiped out his money and as her mother was a homemaker, there was no income coming in to offset them.

Carrie offered to sell her boutique to help out, but her

father refused. He hadn't beaten the cancer, but his life insurance policy had at least allowed her mother to keep the house she'd lived in for the last thirty years. Carrie promised herself then though that she would be richer than her father. She wasn't sure a billion dollars would protect her from facing the same fate, but it made her feel better.

The bell above the door jingled and she looked up and smiled. Philippe stood in the doorway. He flashed her a wicked, sexy smile and strode her direction.

"Are you ready for dinner, Chéri?" She loved his French accent and the fact he called her Chéri. It didn't hurt that he was devastatingly handsome either.

"Yes, just let me grab my purse." Carrie folded the paper and shoved it in the drawer under her register. She would have to show Gwen later and thank her.

After ducking into the back room to grab her bag and coat, she stopped by the sewing room to inform Sierra and the new hires she was leaving for the night. Then she returned and linked her arm through Philippe's.

"Where are we going tonight?" Carrie asked as they stepped out into the crisp evening air. Winter seemed to be hanging around a lot longer this year though no more snow was predicted. Carrie longed for spring. She detested winter, except for Christmas of course. Maybe it was because she got cold too easily or perhaps it was her love of wearing short sleeves and skirts - neither of which were practical in the cold New England winters.

"Someplace special." He opened the door of his silver BMW for her and she slid in relishing the feel of the leather seats. While she enjoyed having a driver, she liked that Philippe drove his own car. Sometimes it was nice to do things for yourself. She hoped that wouldn't change now that she was officially a billionaire. Though they were trying to break the stereotypes, Gwen often shared some of the crazy requirements that Drew faced as a billionaire.

"Oh, yeah? What's the occasion?" Carrie didn't dare to hope that he would be proposing - it was probably still too soon - but that would be a nice occasion. Philippe seemed to fit the bill of the perfect man in her head, and while most of her relationships lasted a month or less, she could envision herself with Philippe. He was driven, nice, and he attended church with her.

"You'll see," he said and flashed her a wink as he started the car.

A few minutes later, they pulled into an upscale Italian restaurant. Carrie bit her lip as disappointment surged through her. While she loved Italian food, she avoided it most of the time to keep her trim figure. Philippe knew that, or she thought he did. Plus, he was French. Why wouldn't he take her to a French restaurant? Well, she supposed the restaurant would have a salad.

"Come on," he said as he turned off the ignition and opened his door.

Carrie's lips pulled into a tight smile as she unbuckled her seatbelt. She pushed open her side and took his hand when he offered it.

Philippe held the restaurant door open, and they stepped into the quaint building. The sweet smell of tomatoes and garlic and bread floated on the air. Carrie tried not to inhale too deeply. Just sniffing bread always seemed to put five pounds on her. Instead, she focused on the intricate artwork on the wall that displayed a vineyard and an Italian chateau. The designer had even added lines to make it appear cracked and faded giving it a charming vintage look.

"Hello, we have reservations under Caron," Philippe said as he approached the hostess, a smart looking blond in black pants and a pressed white shirt.

"Very good, sir. Follow me." She led the way toward the back of the restaurant to a small booth lit by candlelight and a small lamp attached to the wall. Curtains hung around the booth giving it an extra measure of privacy.

"This is nice," Carrie said as they sat. The hostess handed them menus and then as if sensing they wanted to be alone, she turned and walked away.

"Only the best for my girl." He took her hand and stared into her eyes.

"Ah, that's sweet."

"I hope it's enough. It's my first time dating a billionaire." He flashed her a crooked smile as if he were teasing, but there was a seriousness behind his words like he believed she required different treatment.

More than that though were the words themselves. She had just found out her net worth today and had told no one. So how did he know? "Who said I'm a billionaire?" Carrie asked as she pulled her hand back and took a sip of her water.

For a moment, his face held the expression of a child caught with his hand in the cookie jar. Then it shifted and a genuine smile lit his features. "Well, I understand business has picked up since the article on you ran, and you are such an amazing designer that I can't believe you aren't there already. I presume you will be soon."

Relief flooded Carrie. Would it always be like this? Would she second guess everyone's intentions? "That's very nice of you to say, but I owe my success mostly to Gwen. It was her wearing my designs that got me noticed."

He took a sip of his water. "Yes, it's good to have wealthy friends, but you were on your way there before Gwen."

Philippe couldn't know that since he entered her life after Gwen had started wearing her designs, but it was sweet of him to say. And she probably would have gotten there herself, but having Gwen wear her wedding dress had shot her up the ladder faster than she had imagined. Still, she didn't want to talk money with Philippe. Perhaps it was a baseless fear, but Carrie needed to know he wanted to be with her for her and not for her money.

"Thank you, but let's talk of something else. How is business for you going?"

Philippe ran a computer consulting firm. They helped businesses choose the best computers for their needs, aided in setting up their systems, and repaired them when needed. Philippe wasn't hurting for money either which was another thing Carrie liked about him. The fact that he made his own money made her less wary of him being after hers. But, she believed her worth was higher than his, and she knew that bothered some men. He never said anything, but she'd known many men in the past who hid their feelings behind calm exteriors until they finally exploded.

"Can't complain. Business is going well."

The waitress appeared then and placed a basket of bread in the middle of the table. "Are you ready to order?"

Carrie opened her mouth to ask for more time - she hadn't even surveyed the menu - but Philippe spoke before her words formed.

"We'll both have the Tour of Italy and two glasses of red wine," Philippe said.

Carrie stared at him incredulously. He had never

ordered for her before and she didn't appreciate it now. "Um, I don't feel like pasta tonight. I'll just have whatever salad you recommend." She locked eyes with the waitress to convey her seriousness.

The waitress's eyebrow rose as she scratched the order out on her pad. "Okay. Anything else?"

"Sorry, I thought since it was a special occasion-" Philippe began.

"It's fine," Carrie said interrupting him. Although it wasn't fine. She probably wouldn't mind his ordering for her if he took her dietary needs into consideration, but he hadn't even consulted her or asked what she wanted. "I'm simply craving salad is all."

"All right, a salad for the lady and the Tour of Italy for me. Also a bottle of your best red wine."

"Of course, sir." The waitress hightailed it from their table as if she couldn't wait to escape the tension.

A silence fell. Philippe grabbed a piece of bread from the basket. Carrie was tempted to as well, but she'd just put her foot down about pasta; she'd feel like a hypocrite if she did. Still, she wished she had something to chew on to fill the heavy silence.

Philippe finished his bite and then looked at her. He cleared his throat. "I was going to wait for dessert, but perhaps this is the right time." His hand reached into his pocket, and he pulled out a box. "I know we haven't been seeing each other that long, Carrie, but I love you. And my heart tells me you are the woman for me. Would you do me the honor of being my wife?" Philippe flicked open the box, and Carrie stared at the ring.

A thousand different things ran through her mind: they hadn't been dating long enough, the ring was beautiful, why hadn't he gotten down on one knee, did she love him? But none of them were the real reason that gave her pause. That was a secret she had told no one. Yet.

*C*al stared at the piece of wood in his hands. Usually, inspiration hit him as soon as he held the block of wood, but this time it was slow in coming. It was probably the stress from the lack of money. He'd managed to get an extension with the bank, but it was simply plugging a hole to slow the leak and not stopping it entirely.

"You know, you could sell some of your carvings as a side job." Stacy set a mug of coffee on the table next to him.

"That's what I told him," Jim, Stacy's husband, said from across the room. "I'm sure I would sell a ton of them at the store." Jim and Stacy owned the general store in Soda Spurs. She did the books for both the store and his ranching business while Jim ran the day-to-day operations.

"Plus, I bet you could make an online store and sell

them there too." Stacy sat on the other side of the couch Cal occupied. "Isn't that what everyone does nowadays? Set up stores and sell things online?"

"Maybe some do, but I wouldn't even know where to begin." Cal turned the wood over in his hand again. Maybe a horse. He could whittle a horse like Ginger or perhaps a dog like Dexter.

"I bet Ginny would help you with that," Stacy pushed, "I've heard she's pretty computer savvy. Just another reason you guys would complement each other so perfectly."

Cal glared at his sister. "Stacy, we've been over this. I'm not interested in Ginny, and I'm not going to use her for her money or her computer skills."

Stacy's shoulders pulled back in a defensive posture. "I'm only trying to help."

"I know, but I'm not ready yet." Cal brought the knife to the wood and scraped off a sliver of wood. He wished he was. He wanted to start a family soon, but right now his heart still belonged to the fiery red head who had stolen it six years ago. It wouldn't be fair to date any other woman seriously until he could give her his whole heart. Cal just wondered when he would ever be able to do that.

With a sigh, Stacy turned her attention to her husband and they caught up on the rest of the day's events. This time, after dinner and after the kids had gone to bed was their best time to share about their day and Cal often felt like he was intruding. His knife continued to scrape against the wood, and he wasn't surprised when the image that began to appear was the heart- shaped face of the woman he could never seem to get out of his head.

CHAPTER 4

"*P*hilippe proposed?" Gwen's eyes shot to Carrie's hand. Disbelief filled her voice.

Carrie glanced down at the large diamond ring on her left hand. It still felt foreign and not completely right. "Yeah."

Gwen's brow furrowed sending tiny crinkle lines across her forehead. "You don't seem excited."

"No, I am, it's just that..." Carrie bit her lip. She had shared most of her past with Gwen, but there was one tidbit she had never told her - never told anyone.

"What?" Gwen asked. Concern replaced the shock and Gwen leaned across the table to give Carrie her full attention. Carrie loved that about Gwen, how effortlessly her emotions shifted.

Carrie's eyes fell to the floor and she studied the

speckled flooring of her kitchen as she tried to formulate the words in her mind, "There's something I never told you. It happened before we met, and it... well it's embarrassing."

Gwen chuckled and leaned back in the chair. "Embarrassing? This is me you're talking to, remember? I'm the one who spilled water on my future mother-in-law at a high brow gala. I should have a degree in embarrassing."

Carrie was glad that money hadn't changed Gwen. She was still the same warm, caring person she had always been. "Yeah, but that was water. Nothing permanent. Trust me, this is much worse."

An impish expression stole across Gwen's face, and she wiggled her eyebrows. "What? Do you have some criminal past I am unaware of? Let me guess. You got caught streaking across campus your freshman year."

"No, nothing like that," Carrie said with a laugh. "At least I hope not. There were a few parties before I met you that are a little hazy, but I would remember that, right?"

Gwen's eyebrow arched, and Carrie chuckled. "I'm kidding."

"Okay," Gwen shrugged, "so if you're not a closet streaker, I doubt you have anything to worry about."

Carrie sighed. She didn't know about that, but she did need her best friend's advice. She took a deep breath and spilled it out. "So, on my twenty-first birthday, some friends and I flew out to Vegas. We got drunk, of course, I mean that's what you do in Vegas when you're twenty-one, right?"

"I wouldn't know," Gwen said softly.

Carrie blinked at her. Had the girl never had a wild side? She realized Gwen had lived a simpler life, but had she never let loose? Carrie shook her head to clear the rabbit trail thoughts. "Right, well anyway, I guess I was so out of it that I sort of... got married." Carrie's gaze dropped to the tabletop as the heat crawled up her neck.

"Wait, you sort of did what?" Gwen's eyes grew to the size of quarters, and she leaned farther across the table.

"I know," Carrie moaned as she dropped her head onto her hand. "It was crazy and wrong and and I barely even knew the man, but I guess I thought I felt something there. I agreed to marry him, and the next morning when I woke up, he was there."

Gwen's eyes softened. "Okay, I mean mistakes happen, but are you sure it was even legal? A lot of people think they get legally married in Vegas, but they really don't."

"No, I remember getting the marriage certificate before we went to the chapel. They still require a certificate, but you can get it within an hour. No three-day waiting period in Vegas." Carrie raised her head. "Why is there no three-day waiting period in Vegas?"

A soft chuckle escaped Gwen's lips. "Well, probably because people want to get married quickly. But, why didn't you get it annulled? You could have done that the next morning. Claimed insanity or something."

Carrie shook her head. "I... I don't know. I've asked myself that same question many times over the years. I do remember asking him that first morning, but he said we belonged together, and he wouldn't agree. I couldn't convince him, so I think I just convinced myself it hadn't happened, and then I guess I forgot about it for a while, but now it's an issue. I won't be able to get a marriage license as long as I'm still married."

"Do you remember his name? Anything else?" Gwen crossed to the stove and set the kettle boiling. Evidently, she felt this conversation needed tea.

"His name is Cal Roper. He lives in a small town in Texas - Soda Pop or something like that."

A small smile played across Gwen's lips as she crossed to the pantry. "That seems like a lot to remember from one night six years ago. Just how do you know where he lives?"

Busted. Carrie cleared her throat. "Hang on."

Gwen turned from the pantry, an inquisitive look on her face and the box of green tea in her hand.

Carrie rose from the table and walked down the hall to her room. On the top shelf of her closet was an innocuous red shoe box. Any person who looked in her closet would simply think it was a pair of shoes she hadn't unpacked. Goodness knew she had enough of them, but that wasn't what the box contained. She pulled the box down and took a deep breath before opening the lid. Inside were six plump envelopes. One for every year she and Cal had been married.

She wasn't even sure why she had kept the letters. Maybe it was to reminisce. Every once in a while, she would pull them down and read over them. Maybe it was to remind her not to be so spontaneous in the future. Whatever the reason, she had them and she was about to share them with another person for the first time.

Carrie took a deep breath and returned to the kitchen. She set the box on the table and glanced at Gwen whose face still held a quizzical expression. "I know all that information because he writes me every year on our anniversary."

"Is that why you get so weird around your birthday?" Gwen opened the cupboard that held the mugs. She grabbed two and placed them on the counter near the stove.

Carrie nodded and picked up a letter. "Every year, I get a card from him a few days before my birthday. He tells me it wasn't a mistake, and he asks me to come see him." She slipped the letter out of the envelope and scanned the slanted writing.

"Carrie," Gwen's voice was soft, like a gentle caress, "Do you think maybe Cal is why you can't settle down with anyone?" She dropped a tea bag in each mug and leaned against the counter.

"What?" Carrie's jaw dropped open, and she shook her head. "No way. I don't belong with Cal. He's…. he's a cowboy on a ranch somewhere. He's probably dirty all the time. Can you imagine me on a ranch with animals?"

"Well, I've never thought about it, but love can change people. I would never have imagined myself marrying a billionaire, but it happened."

"Yeah, but that's totally different, Gwen. You're in love with Drew. You two belong together. I was young and stupid and-"

"And you've never done anything about it." Carrie opened her mouth to protest, but Gwen held up her hand. "I'm just saying that maybe there is a reason you never did anything about it. Maybe there's a reason you don't stick with men very long. Maybe there's a reason you've kept every letter he mailed you. Maybe this Cal holds more of your heart than you want to admit."

"But, but it was just one night." Even as she said the words, Carrie wondered if Gwen might be right.

Her longest relationship after that night in Vegas had been two months until Philippe. She always found some reason to stop dating the men. They were too stiff, they were too free-spirited, they didn't make enough, they worked too many hours. But she couldn't really be comparing them to Cal, could she? What did she even remember about Cal?

She remembered twinkling green eyes and a charming smile. She remembered the cutest dimple in his right cheek and the way his arms felt around her as they danced across the floor. Oh, dear. Did she really have unresolved feelings for Cal? No, those were just physical characteristics. He had been handsome, but so what? Philippe was handsome too, and she loved him. Didn't she? She glanced down at the diamond on her left hand, but suddenly she wasn't so sure.

"Sometimes one night is all it takes," Gwen said with a slight shrug of her shoulders. "I knew after one night with Drew that something was there. I was just too stubborn to do anything about it at first." She cocked an eyebrow. "Perhaps stubbornness is a trait we share."

The tea kettle whistled then halting the conversation for a moment as Gwen turned off the kettle and poured the water into the two mugs. She handed one to Carrie and blew softly into her own. "So, when are you going down there?"

"Soon," Carrie said with a small sigh. "I have to remedy the situation. Hopefully Sierra can run the store while I'm gone." Sierra had been her assistant for three months and knew her way around the shop. In addition, Carrie had hired Lilly to answer the phones and take orders and Devyn who was a whiz with the sewing machine and could whip out Carrie's designs in a few days.

"I'm sure she will have no problem doing that," Gwen said. She set her cup down on the table and picked up an envelope.

"Yeah, this just isn't how I thought I'd be celebrating," Carrie said.

"Well, you can still celebrate. Have you told Philippe?"

"No, and I'm not sure I want to." Carrie had been pondering what to tell Philippe since the night before. How did she tell her fiancé that she had to go get divorced before they could marry?

Gwen pulled the letter from the envelope and scanned the contents. "If you don't tell him the truth, what will you say?"

Carrie didn't miss the disapproving tone in Gwen's voice. "I don't know. Maybe just that I have some business to take care of. It certainly wouldn't be a lie."

Gwen set the letter down and fixed Carrie with a knowing stare. "No, but it wouldn't be the whole truth either, and you know how things can spiral out of control when there're secrets."

"I know. I know," Carrie said shaking her head. She'd figure out what to say to Philippe later. Right now, she just wanted to change the conversation. "The engagement wasn't really what I was talking about celebrating though."

"You have more to celebrate?"

Carrie chuffed softly glad that the letters had been forgotten for now. "I made it into the billionaire's club."

Gwen's mouth fell open. "What? That's terrific, Carrie. I know you've wanted it for ages."

"Well, I have you to thank. That article and the picture of you wearing my wedding dress got me noticed. I didn't think it would happen that quickly, but I got the notice from my accountant yesterday that I'm officially a billionaire."

"That's wonderful, Carrie." Gwen's eyes sparkled as she set her mug down and squeezed Carrie's arm. Then her features shifted. "Did you... did you tell Philippe?"

"Not exactly. The paper came before he picked me up and I didn't say anything about it, but he did mention dating a billionaire at dinner." She narrowed her eyes at Gwen. "Why do you ask?"

Gwen's eyes slid to the ground. "I don't know. I don't want to speak ill about him as I don't know him as well as you do, but I just wonder at the timing of it."

Anger flared within Carrie. "You think he's only asked me to marry him to get my money?"

Gwen shook her head. "I didn't say that, but you two haven't been dating long."

"Drew proposed to you after only a few months." Carrie knew she was being defensive, but she couldn't help it. Gwen had hit on the very insecurity Carrie had been struggling with. She liked Philippe, but she also wondered at his timing and his slip of the tongue the night before. "Besides, Philippe has his own money."

"I'm sure you're right." Gwen picked up her mug again and kept her eyes focused on the liquid. "Dating Drew has made me a little cynical about people's intentions I fear."

"It comes with the territory," Carrie said softening her tone as well. She'd dealt with the fear that people only liked her for her money all her life, and she knew Gwen, because she was new to it, was just looking out for her.

"Did Cal know about your money?" Gwen asked.

"Well, I wasn't as wealthy then," Carrie began, but she thought back to that weekend. Most of it was fuzzy, but she had no memory of telling Cal about her money. "I don't think I told him though."

"Well, that's something then."

"What is?" Carrie asked. She wasn't following Gwen's train of thought.

She picked up the folded piece of paper again. "This is romantic, Carrie, and I imagine the others are similar. If he didn't know about your money, then I'd wager he has real feelings for you. Why else would he write you every year for six years even though you never write back?"

Carrie bit her lip as Gwen's words sunk in. If she hadn't mentioned the money, why would Cal want to stay married to her? Why would he write her year after year with no reply? Could it be that he had really fallen for her?

CHAPTER 5

"What do you mean you have to go to Texas?" Philippe asked as he crossed his arms. This stiff almost angry posture was unlike him.

Carrie bit the inside of her lip. She hated lying, but she didn't think telling Philippe the whole truth right now would be a good thing. So, she'd opted for the lie of omission. "I told you, I have some business to take care of."

"Business in Texas? Have you ever even been to Texas, Carrie?"

He didn't believe her, and she had clearly aroused his suspicion, but there was nothing to do now but carry on the lie. "I have a friend there."

His jaw clenched. "A friend? Carrie, we just got

engaged. Shouldn't we be planning a wedding or something?"

Well, at least he hadn't asked who the friend was. "We have plenty of time for that, Philippe. I promise. Drew's letting me take the charter jet. That will cut back on the time, and I'll be back before you know it. Probably by tomorrow night."

"I don't like the idea of you traveling alone. Why don't I come with you?"

Carrie twitched as the thought ran through her head. That could be the worst idea ever. She had no idea if Cal had changed at all, but the two men in the same room would more than likely just turn into a competition if not a full-fledged fist fight. "You have work," she said shaking her head. "Didn't you just take on a new company?"

Philippe's face twisted and Carrie figured he knew she was right, but he was trying to come up with another option. "Fine," he finally said. The words came out more like a sigh than a statement. "But please keep me informed of your journey and progress."

Another prick pinged Carrie's conscience. She had no intention of telling him her progress, but she could update him on her arrival. "I will."

Though he didn't look entirely satisfied, he accepted her kiss and stepped back. Carrie couldn't help but notice the worry lines still etched in his face as she walked past him to Gwen and Drew who stood at the bottom of the stairs leading into the plane.

"Thank you for letting me take the private plane," Carrie said to Drew. "I suppose I could have chartered my own-"

"Nonsense." He held up a hand cutting her off. "There's no sense chartering a second one when I have this plane and no reason to deal with airport issues when you have a plane at your disposal. Now, there's no airport in Soda Spurs, so you'll be landing about an hour away."

"That's fine," Carrie said. "I'd rather keep a low profile anyway. No sense causing a scene."

"So, do you have a plan?" Gwen asked in a quiet voice. Undoubtedly, she'd told Drew the real story, but Carrie had asked her not to tell Philippe. At least not yet. Gwen hadn't been happy, but she'd agreed it was Carrie's story to tell when she was ready.

A plan. Carrie had thought all night about how best to handle the situation but come up with nothing. Would Cal fight her? She hoped he would change his mind about wanting to marry her when he saw her again, sign the papers, and let her be on her way, but she doubted it would be that easy. Whatever he did, she figured honesty would be the best option. "I'm just going to show up and ask him to sign the papers."

"And what if he doesn't?" Gwen asked.

Carrie understood Gwen was just playing devil's

advocate, but it annoyed her nonetheless. "He has to. I'm going to ask nicely. Bribe him if I have to." Gwen shot her an incredulous stare, but Carrie wasn't kidding. "I am not sure what I'll do if he doesn't."

Gwen squeezed her arm and flashed a sympathetic smile, but it didn't lessen Carrie's worries. What would she do if Cal refused?

*D*exter's ears perked and his head turned toward the barn entrance. A soft whine escaped his throat. Cal had heard nothing, but Dexter, who possessed much better hearing, obviously had.

"What is it boy?" Cal asked as he led Ginger from the stall.

Dexter's response was a sharp bark and a tail wag. His eyes never wavered from the barn door.

"All right, let's go check it out." Cal tugged on Ginger's reigns to get her moving. As they stepped out of the barn and back into the open air, the crunch of tires on gravel reached Cal's ears. He checked his watch. Stacy usually returned at day's end to check on everything, but it wasn't quite that time yet, and he wasn't expecting anyone else. Surely it wouldn't be the bank wanting payment on the loan yet. He had told them he was working on something and they generally left him alone as long as he delivered.

Dexter barked again and pranced around Cal's legs as if urging him to hurry or give permission to run ahead.

"Go on then," Cal said giving him permission. "I'll secure Ginger and I'll be right there."

Dexter's head bobbed as if agreeing with a nod. People said dogs didn't talk, but Dexter seemed to be an exception to that rule. He gave one final glance at Cal and then bounded toward the front of the house.

Cal shook his head as he tied Ginger's reins to the corral. That dog was sometimes more human than canine. Before he made it around the side of his house, a feminine scream carried through the air, and Cal quickened his pace, wondering what Dexter had done now.

When he rounded the corner, he pulled up short and bit his lips to keep from laughing at the scene in front of him. A mid-sized sedan he didn't recognize sat parked in front of his house. Dexter had pinned the driver to her door and was attempting to sniff or lick her face - it wasn't clear from Cal's position. What he could discern was that the woman was actively trying to avoid Dexter's tongue. Her red mane swished from side to side as her face darted to the left and right. Wait, red hair? Could it be? The lingering sunlight picked up the copper in her hair and Cal thought back to the first time his eyes saw the beautiful color.

"Will someone get this mangy mutt off me?"

Cal's breath caught. Though it had been years, that

voice was burned into his memory. Coupled with the coppery red hair, it could be no one else. Carrie Bliss was in his driveway.

"Dexter, down," he called when he found his voice again. The dog whined but dropped to the ground and returned to Cal's side.

"You really should teach that dog some manners," she said as she wiped at her white jacket. The remnants of dusty paw prints remained even after her hands finished.

Cal crossed his arms and leaned against the porch post. "He's just excited. We don't get a lot of visitors and no one we know wears all white to a ranch."

Her posture stiffened a moment at the sound of his voice. Then she turned around and caught his gaze, her emerald eyes fierce and resolute. "Hi, Cal."

Two words. That's all she said, but that was all it took. Immediately he was transported back to Vegas.

He had been there attending a friend's bachelor party and while everyone else pounded enough liquor to become stupid drunk, Cal had only partaken of one beer. He wasn't really a fan of the taste, and he didn't like the feeling of being out of control.

"Dude, go ask some girl to dance," his friend John said with a slur.

"I'm good, really." Cal was honestly hoping the party would end soon. Fatigue covered him, and he just wanted to crawl into bed, but it would be rude to leave this early.

"No, you're not. You're not having any fun. You're barely drinking, so go find a girl. Look, there's a perfect one."

Cal followed John's finger not expecting much. His friend was three sheets to the wind at least, but as the sea of people parted briefly, Cal's heart paused in his chest. A beautiful red headed woman surrounded by a few friends danced freely to the music. Her body swayed in perfect time to the beat, and a smile stretched across her lips as if the dance floor made her feel alive. She was the most exotic, intoxicating woman he had ever seen.

His feet propelled him across the room though he had no idea what he would say to her. When nothing brilliant came to mind, he said the first thing he thought of. "Hi, I'm Cal, and I think you're beautiful."

Her eyes flicked to his and the corners of her mouth pulled into a flirtatious grin. She closed the space between and splayed her hands across his chest. "Hi Cal," she said as she looked up at him with sparkly green eyes.

"Are you just going to stand there all day?"

The harsh tone in Carrie's words drug him back to the present, and Cal shook his head to clear the cobwebs of the past away. "How you been, Carrie?"

A tight smile played across Carrie's lips. "I've been better, Cal." She walked around the front of the car toward him. Physically, she looked the same, but there was a difference in her. She seemed stiffer, more polished. Her white jacket was tailored perfectly to her form as were her pants, and the emerald shirt that skirted her neckline brought out the same color in her eyes. She was a vision of perfection. "But you can help." She held out a stapled packet to him. "I need you to sign these."

He took the papers though he knew what they were. Only divorce papers would bring her all the way out to him. Cal scanned the papers - he had no plans to sign them, but she didn't need to know that. "Why now?"

Carrie bit her lip and her eyes fell to the ground. "I should have done it ages ago, but I just kept ignoring it. However, I can't ignore it any longer because..." she lifted her left hand, "because I'm getting married. He's a wonderful man and this time I'm ready to be married, but I can't do that until we get divorced."

Cal searched her eyes. She did seem earnest and sincere, but she'd never given their love a chance, and he wasn't ready to give her up without a fight. "I'll make you a deal," he said crossing his arms. "You stay here for a few days and give us a chance. If, at the end of that time, you still want a divorce, I'll sign the papers."

Her eyes flashed, and a spark of the old Carrie reappeared. "No, I'm not dating another man while I'm engaged. That's not right."

"Technically, you already have been." His gaze never wavered. He might still lose, depending on how stubborn she was, but at least this gave him a chance.

"But that's... that's not the same thing. We barely knew each other. We were both inebriated-"

"I wasn't drunk," he said cutting her off. "I was very aware of what I was doing. I knew from the moment I saw you that I felt something and when you said my name and put your hands on my chest, I knew I wanted to marry you. And you can claim intoxication all you want, but you were pretty firm in your decision that night as well."

"I…" Carrie opened her mouth but her words stalled. She held his gaze for a minute before pinching her lips together. A tiny vein throbbed in her clenched jaw, and Cal had to bite back a smile at how cute she looked when she was angry.

Cal raised a brow and tilted his head to the side. "It's either stay the few days or we stay married."

Irritation flared on Carrie's face sending a red flush up her neck. "What do you even hope to get out of this, Cal?"

He locked eyes with her. "You."

CHAPTER 6

*C*arrie blinked as the wave of emotions rolled over her. Flattery hit first. That he would still want her after all this time was ego boosting, but it was followed quickly with disbelief. Why would he still want her after all this time unless he was after her money? Indignation flared soon after. How dare he barter with her life as if it meant nothing! She had a fiancé back home whom she loved or at least thought she loved, and she should not be staying here with this practically perfect stranger. It didn't matter that they were married on paper; she knew almost nothing about him.

Carrie returned his frank stare as she weighed her options. He had her between a rock and a hard place. She couldn't very well leave and stay married so that left staying. "Fine, but I'm not staying here. It wouldn't be proper. This town has a hotel, right?"

A deep, irritating chuckle spilled from Cal's lips. "A hotel? No, but there is an inn, and since there's no festival going on this weekend, you might find a vacancy. I do have plenty of room here though-"

"Not on your life," Carrie seethed. "I'll take my chances on the inn. Do you have an address?"

"Nah, but I can take you there. You could get settled in and then come back here for a bit. I'll make you dinner and show you around."

None of that sounded appealing to Carrie, but as she was at his mercy, at least for the time being, she agreed. "Fine, get in. You can lead the way, but I'm driving."

Cal tipped his hat at her before pushing himself off the railing and sauntering to the sedan. The way he confidently carried himself was sexy and Carrie watched him fold his long frame into the passenger seat before shaking her head and crossing back to the driver's side. This was not what she had planned at all, and she had no business thinking of him as sexy. That was a rabbit trail she should not go down.

"This is nice," Cal said as she started the engine. His hand glided down the leather seat beneath him.

"It's a rental," Carrie said, "but thanks. Now where are we going?"

Cal removed his hat and pointed straight ahead. "You drive, and I'll tell you when to turn."

Carrie swallowed her irritation and shifted into drive. A few minutes later, they pulled up in front of a quaint two-story home. "You sure this is an inn?" Carrie asked. "I mean other than the sign, it looks more like a house."

"Well, that's the charm of Soda Spurs. It's got that home-grown vibe."

The corners of Cal's lips pulled up into an irresistibly charming smile. *Darn it. Why did he have to be handsome?* This would be so much easier if she felt no attraction to him.

"Right." She pulled her eyes from his face and turned off the ignition. "Let's see if there's any room at the inn then."

"The sign said Vacancy, so I think you're good," Cal said as he opened his car door.

Before she even had her seatbelt off, he was opening the driver's side door for her.

"I can open my own door," she said. Did he think she was incapable or weak?

"I'm sure you can," he took off his cowboy hat and flashed her a wink, "but my momma raised me right, and it's only fitting I open the door for my wife."

"I'm not your-" Carrie trailed off at the teasing glint in his eye. She would not win this particular argument with him, so she might as well stop trying. "Fine, thank you."

He placed the hat back on his head and tapped the

brim at her. "You're very welcome. Shall we head inside then?"

"Unless you want to stand outside all day." Carrie poured enough vitriol in her voice to garner an eyebrow raise from Cal.

"Nah, no sense in that. Momma would have my hide if I left you to wilt out here." He glanced toward the trunk. "Do you have bags I can help with?"

"No need," Carrie said. "I hadn't planned on staying long, so I only have one bag. I'm certain I can manage to carry that." She punctuated her words with sharp steps to the trunk of the car. Her heels made a satisfying clacking sound on the pavement. When she reached the back, she punched the button on the remote, staring at Cal as it popped open. Then, she pulled out her bag before shutting the lid.

He was waiting at the side of the car as she shut the trunk, and he nodded at her before leading the way up the pathway. A tiny bell jingled as he pushed open the front door, and a wave of warmth rolled out to greet them.

"Welcome to the Soda Spurs Inn." The bubbly voice belonged to a short, stout woman with curly brown hair. "Oh, hey, Cal. What can I do for you?"

"Hi, Dixie, this is my friend Carrie, and she needs a room for a few nights."

Relief flooded Carrie that he had called her his friend instead of his wife. Though she would probably never see the people in the town again once she left, she didn't want to explain to everyone her situation with Cal.

"Welcome, Carrie," Dixie said turning her friendly gaze on Carrie. "How long will you be staying?"

Carrie raised a brow and turned to Cal. "That's a good question. Cal?"

His lips twisted into a mischievous smile and he shrugged leaving Carrie on her own.

"At least tonight with the option to extend?"

Dixie looked from Cal to Carrie clearly picking up on something. "Lucky for you, this is not a busy time. I can certainly do that for you, and you can tell me each night if you'll be checking out the next morning or not."

"Thank you. That sounds perfect." Carrie would have preferred to be on the jet already heading back, but as that wasn't possible, she would make the best of the situation.

"Great. Well, let me show you to your room." Dixie grabbed a key from the rack behind her.

"I'll wait here." Cal nodded at Dixie and then wandered over to an open chair.

"So, what brought you to Soda Spurs?" Dixie asked as she led the way up the stairs.

"Cal did, actually. We met each other a few years ago, and now I need a favor from him." Carrie hoped that explanation would be enough to satisfy Dixie's curiosity.

"Oh, I'm sure he will do whatever you need. Cal is the sweetest man, but I'm sure I don't have to tell you that."

Dixie inserted the key into the door and opened it to reveal a small room decorated in a soft rose color. "It's not huge, but it has a private bath and a closet," Dixie said gesturing to the door on the right side of the room.

"It's fine, thank you," Carrie said. "I didn't bring much anyway."

"All right. Well, don't hesitate to call me if you need anything at all. If I don't have it here, I can tell you where to get it." Dixie flashed a final sweet smile before turning and exiting the room.

When the door closed behind her, Carrie walked to the bed and placed her small bag on top. She had brought little, hoping to only spend a day or two in town, but she should probably unpack what was folded in her overnight bag to keep it from getting too wrinkled.

Before she did that though, she needed to call Philippe and inform him of her arrival, so he wouldn't worry.

The phone rang four times in her ear before going to voicemail. As she listened to his announcement, she wondered what he was doing that kept him from answering the phone. It was nearing eight pm back in New York and he rarely worked that late. "Hey, Philippe, I made it to Texas. It looks like it might take a few days to finish up my business, but I rented a nice room. I guess you are working late, so I'll try you again later. Bye."

Carrie ended the call and then dialed Gwen. At least

talking to her might lighten Carrie's mood. Unlike Philippe, Gwen picked up on the first ring.

"Hey, Carrie, how is it going?"

"Not well," Carrie said. "Cal is still refusing to sign. He wants me to spend a few days here and then he said he'll sign if I haven't changed my mind. He has some nerve." Carrie shoved clothes in the dresser drawer as she seethed and then turned to the closet to hang the few items that needed it. She shouldn't care about wrinkles. Cal and Dixie both wore jeans and plaid shirts, so they probably didn't care about her wrinkles, and maybe if she came across as a slob, Cal would decide he didn't want her and sign the stupid papers. No, she wouldn't do that. Even if it might work, Carrie could never handle looking like a slob.

"I think it's kind of romantic," Gwen said softly from the other side of the phone.

Carrie stopped unpacking long enough to hold the phone out and stare at the screen. She knew Gwen couldn't see her, but she couldn't believe those words would come out of her mouth. "Whose side are you on anyway?"

"Yours, but you have to admit, Carrie, it's like a Hallmark movie. This guy has held a torch for you for six years and all he wants is one last ditch effort to win you over."

"But I'm engaged to Philippe." Why did no one seem to understand that?

"But should you be?"

Carrie shook her head and placed her toothbrush on the bathroom counter. Had Gwen lost her mind? "Should I be? Of course, I should be. He asked, and I said yes. That's all there is to it."

Gwen sighed in Carrie's ear. "Do you hear yourself, Carrie? You didn't even say you loved him."

Irritation flared inside Carrie. "Yes, I love him. I wouldn't have said yes if I didn't love him." Would she have? All of a sudden, she wasn't so sure. Carrie sank onto the bed and dropped her head onto her hands. "This is such a mess."

"Or a message." Gwen's soft voice held no condemnation. "Sometimes there are reasons we do things. Maybe you never divorced Cal because you had feelings for him even if you didn't realize it. Maybe this is God's way of giving you both a second chance."

"I think you have newlywed brain," Carrie said with a shake of her head. "It was one stupid night six years ago. I'm not supposed to be with him. He's just being stubborn, but two can play at that game." She stood and smoothed her shirt. "In fact, I think I will go have another word with him."

"Okay," Gwen said with a sigh. "I hope you know what you're doing."

"I do know what I'm doing. I'm doing what I came here to do. I'll keep you informed." Carrie hung up the phone, pulled back her shoulders, and yanked open the door. This was crazy. She had married Cal on a whim, not because she cared for him, and she was going to remind him of that.

Cal stood as she entered the foyer, his black Stetson in his hands. "You all good?"

"Yeah, I think so."

"Ready for the tour then?"

Carrie rolled her eyes. As if she had much choice in the matter. "Sure, why not?"

They loaded back up in her car, and Carrie drove back to Cal's ranch. Though the drive was quiet, she couldn't help sneaking sideways glances at him. He'd been handsome six years ago, but the dark stubble on his cheeks added to his look giving him a rugged masculinity which sent her heart thumping. She tightened her grip on the wheel and forced her eyes to stay on the road and off his face.

When they arrived back at his house, Cal again rushed around to open her door before leading her up the front porch steps. "Welcome to casa Roper," Cal said as he held the door open for her.

Carrie stepped into a warm living room decorated simply in blue and browns. The furniture was wooden and appeared handmade, but the cushions had obviously been given to Cal as they didn't match. Still, though the room was clearly decorated by a bachelor, it had a homey feel to it.

A large fireplace filled the left wall and above the mantle was a portrait of a beautiful sunset. Carrie's eyes scanned the room, but no television hung on any wall or sat on any surface. Instead, there was the portrait, a cross, and some pictures. Interesting, but she assumed he had a television in his bedroom or in another room of the house. Philippe had three - one in his living room, one in his bedroom, and one in his kitchen. In fact, Carrie couldn't name a man who didn't have at least one.

"The living room is simple, and it could use a woman's decorating hand, but it's home." Cal flashed a wink at her and Carrie bristled. He was acting as if this was some elaborate game, but it wasn't to her. This was her future.

*C*al continued into his modest kitchen. "Here's the kitchen," he said pointing. "Again, not much, but I'll rustle us up some grub after the ride."

She narrowed her eyes and placed her hands on her slim hips. "So, a drive? To where? No offense, but I didn't see much to experience in this town."

Cal mashed his lips together to keep from smiling.

"Well, there's more than you think, but I wasn't talking about a drive. I said a ride."

Carrie waved her hand. Her fingers were long and slender, feminine. He wondered what they would feel like clasped in his own. "What's the difference?"

A deep chuckle bubbled in his chest, but he didn't feel like sharing just yet. "A lot. You'll see. Come on." He led the way through the kitchen and out the back door.

Dexter looked up from where he had been laying on the porch and rose to his feet, his tail wagging like a metronome.

Carrie stepped back in a cowering gesture. "He won't jump on me again, will he? I'll probably never get all the dirt out of this white as it is."

"Well, you'll learn that wearing white at a ranch isn't the brightest idea, but I'll keep him from jumping on you. At ease, Dexter," Cal said. "Give the lady a chance to warm up to you."

Obediently, Dexter sat back down and stared expectantly at them.

"I think you'll be fine now. Come on."

She flashed the dog another withering stare before straightening and taking a step forward. Her eyes widened as she took in the expansive grounds. "Is all this land yours?" There was a hint of awe in her voice as her eyes scanned the area.

"Everything inside the fences you see. It takes a little land to raise cattle."

"Is that what you do? Raise cattle?"

"Yes ma'am." He offered his hand to help her off the porch as her feet seemed rooted to the spot. Cal wasn't sure if she feared the step or the dirt that would greet her at the bottom.

She stared at his hand a moment before placing hers in his. Though a simple touch, Cal relished the softness of her skin. His own hands were rough from years of hard work outside. Carrie held his hand just until her foot touched the ground and then she dropped it as if a searing flame had erupted from it.

Cal chuckled to himself as he continued to the barn. Ginger was still tied up at the corral, but Carrie would need a horse too, and Mabel would be perfect for her. Dexter joined him but was careful to stay out of the way and farther from Carrie.

"Wait, did you mean ride horses?" Her eyes rounded like half dollars and her mouth fell open.

"Well, I certainly didn't mean ride pigs though Stacy tried that one time. Didn't last too long and by the end of it, she ended up dirtier than the pigs." He laughed at the memory, but Carrie didn't seem to find it quite as funny.

"Who's Stacy?"

"My sister. I've talked about her - both that night in Vegas and in the letters I've written. You have received them, right?" He kept his tone light, but inside he was bursting to find out what she did with those letters. Obviously, she had at least gotten them or else she wouldn't have his address, but had she read them? Thrown them away? Kept them twined with a ribbon in a drawer somewhere? He opened the barn door and stepped in toward Mabel's stall.

"Yes, but Cal I don't ride horses or any animal for that matter."

She had brushed over the information he really wanted, but he didn't press the issue. It would surface later. "Nonsense. You only say that because you never have. This here is Mabel and she's as gentle as they come." He touched the dark mane of hair that flowed down Mabel's neck before turning to grab her saddle.

"I would have no idea how to control her," Carrie said holding up in her hands as if warding off evil.

"You don't have to do much." He placed the saddle pad on Mabel's back and then hoisted the saddle up. Then he reached under her to cinch the front and back girth. Finally, he checked to make sure none of her skin had gotten folded into the cinch. When he was sure she was comfortable and the saddle was secure, he led her out of the stall and toward the barn door. "Mabel here is a good girl. She'll follow whatever Ginger does, and I promise I won't go galloping off on you."

"I'd rather not. The only animal I really like is Gwen's

cat and even then, it's only because I don't have to take care of her. I just cat sit sometimes."

Cal stopped and turned to her. "You cat sit?"

Her face flushed, and her eyes fell to her hands. "It sounds corny I know, but Gwen's my best friend and before she met Drew, she had to work two jobs. I would go to her place and take care of her cat, Tabby."

"Hmm, I've never owned a cat, but I always thought they rather took care of themselves. I mean you put food and water out and change a litter box, right?"

"Well, yes, but Tabby also climbs on my lap and we watch movies together." She glanced up at him, and he couldn't help but chuckle at the serious expression on her face.

"Okay, so why don't you get your own cat?"

"I can't," she said shaking her head and hands at him. "I kill everything. Even houseplants. Gwen once got me a cactus to try to make me feel better, but I killed the cactus. It took a little longer, but I assure you it is dead."

His grin stretched further, and he turned away from her to keep from laughing as he continued toward the corral "I see the problem, but I promise you can't hurt Mabel."

"I'd still rather not take the chance."

He turned back to her, his best hang dog expression on his face. "Come on, Carrie. Let me show you my land and brag a little. You told me back in Vegas that you wanted to see it when I finally did it."

Carrie's brow furrowed. "I did? I have no memory of that conversation."

Cal chuckled to hide the hurt from her words. "Well, it happened. We were talking about what we wanted out of life. You told me your dream of becoming a famous designer, and I told you I wanted to own a large plot of land and ranch. Then you told me that maybe you could design blankets for the cattle to keep them warm." His lips parted in a smile and he shook his head as he replayed the memory. She had been so cute talking about cattle blankets that he hadn't the heart to tell her they wouldn't wear them.

Indecision flooded Carrie's eyes as she looked from Cal to the horse and back again. "Are you sure it's safe?"

"Cross my heart." He signed the X across his chest for good measure.

"All right," she said, "but if I get hurt-"

"I won't let that happen." The teasing lilt dropped from his voice as he spoke the serious words. He would never allow anything to hurt her if he could help it.

Their gazes locked for a moment, and electricity crackled between them. He wanted to kiss her to show her how much he had missed her and how serious he was, but he knew she wouldn't be receptive. Yet. So, he cleared his throat and broke the moment.

"Just put your foot here in the stirrup, and I'll help you up."

She gave him an unsure look but approached the horse. "Like this?" she asked as she lifted her right leg.

"No, left leg in the stirrup. Then you throw your right leg over."

"Cal, I'm not sure-"

"Carrie, it's okay. I've got you." He placed his hands lightly on her hips to reassure her and she stiffened beneath his touch.

"Okay." She lifted her left leg high and managed to get it in the stirrup, but then she lost her balance and fell right into his arms.

Thankfully, Cal had planted his feet, or they might have both ended up in the dirt. He certainly didn't mind Carrie in his embrace, but she was flustered. Her eyes flicked to his and a rose color flooded her cheeks.

"I'm sorry," she said untangling herself from his arms in a hasty effort to escape his touch. "I'll try again."

He applied a little more pressure to her hips to steady her and lifted as she pushed up. After another precarious moment, she swung her right leg around.

"Oh my gosh, did I do it?" A timid smile played on her lips.

"You did. Now hold still so I can adjust your stirrups." He bent down and cinched the stirrups up slightly. Stacy generally rode Mabel and it appeared she was a smidge taller than Carrie.

"What are the stirrups for?" Carrie asked as she wiggled her feet.

"Stability and control. You won't really need them much today other than mounting and dismounting, but if you were galloping, they would be useful to help you stay on the saddle and control Mabel."

He held onto Mabel's reins as he untied Ginger and then mounted as well.

"You make that look so easy," Carrie said.

Cal smiled. "Well, to be fair, I have been doing it a lot longer than you have. I grew up around horses."

"Did your parents own this ranch before you?" Carrie asked as Cal clicked to Ginger and led them in a slow walk toward the field.

"No, this I purchased a few years ago, but my father worked at a stable, so I got to take care of the horses and occasionally ride them. I knew when I was about ten that I wanted to be a rancher. I love being out on a horse, and I can't imagine doing anything else."

"It is pretty out here, but Cal, that's one reason we should end this charade. I'm a city girl. I own a dress shop, and I can't imagine doing anything else either."

Cal glanced at her out of the corner of his eye. He'd had similar thoughts over the years, but God still hadn't given him peace about a divorce. "Where there's an open heart, God will find a way."

Carrie sighed but said nothing more as they continued slowly toward the edge of his property. Cal scanned the area as they rode. The grass was looking thin on this side too. He'd have to look into herding the cattle to the outer field soon to keep them fed. It made his job of monitoring them harder, but at least they would be fed.

"Cal, where do you see me fitting in with all this?" Carrie asked as they turned back to the house.

"Wherever you want to fit in," he said. "Do you have to be in New York to design your clothes?"

"It certainly helps. That is where the high paying customers are. Who would I even sell to out here?"

Her question gave Cal pause. He hadn't really thought about her side. Still, he knew that God could make anything work if people trusted in him, and Cal wasn't willing to give up yet.

CHAPTER 7

*I*t surprised Carrie to see a woman standing on Cal's back porch as they returned. Was she an employee? A friend? She was a nice-looking woman with long brown hair pulled into a ponytail, a red and black flannel shirt, and jeans. A tiny seed of discomfort sprouted in Carrie's stomach. Was that jealousy? Surely not. She didn't want Cal; she was trying to divorce him.

"Well, there you are," she called out when they were close enough. She spoke to Cal, but her eyes were on Carrie. "I was beginning to wonder if I needed to send out a search party."

"And who would head such a party, Sis?" Cal asked as he pulled up on Ginger's reins.

Ah, the sister. Carrie should have known. She could see a little of the resemblance now. The same brown hair and strong nose. His sister didn't have the chiseled features of Cal, but it was clear they shared genes.

"You got me there. I certainly wasn't going to come looking. I was, however, going to ask you if you wanted to come to dinner, but it appears you have a date, so we can do it another time." Was that surprise Carrie heard in the woman's voice?

"Well, not really a date. This is Carrie. She's come to visit." Cal dismounted his horse and turned towards Carrie.

"Not really a visit," Carrie said at the same time his sister said, "Oh."

"Hold on to the horn here," Cal said ignoring Carrie's comment. "Then swing your right leg over. I'll help you down."

Carrie followed his directions and tensed slightly when his hands landed on her waist to steady her descent. She figured it was necessary, and she appreciated the gesture; she simply wished she didn't get tingles from it.

"Carrie? Really?" His sister's expression matched the tone in her voice. "Well, nice to meet you, Carrie." She extended a hand as Carrie approached. "I'm Stacy, Cal's sister."

"Nice to meet you," Carrie said and shook the woman's hand.

"I'll pass on dinner tonight," Cal said coming up

behind Carrie. "I was planning to make chili for Carrie and me."

"You can go have dinner with your family if you want," Carrie said. "I can eat at the inn or somewhere in town and come back tomorrow. You do have restaurants, right?"

"We do. A few, but I'm not leaving you in this town all alone. However, I need to brush down the horses so perhaps Stacy can help start the dinner while I do that?" His voice held a hopeful tone and Carrie recognized the same dogged expression he used on her earlier. He certainly understood how to play to his attributes.

Stacy rolled her eyes, but a smile played across her lips. "I guess if I have to, but you'll owe me."

"Whatever you say, sis." He turned to Carrie. "Go ahead and make yourself at home inside. I'll be there as soon as I finish out here."

Carrie nodded and followed Stacy into the house. "Can you tell me where the bathroom is? I'd like to clean up?"

"Sure, it's right down the hall." Stacy pointed down the hallway before opening the door of the fridge.

Carrie started down the hallway before realizing all the doors were shut. With a pause, she glanced back toward the kitchen knowing she should turn back and ask Stacy which door the bathroom was, but not asking gave her deniability. She probably shouldn't, but curiosity filled Carrie. What was in the other rooms?

She opened the first one to find a home office. A desk, chair, and bookshelf were the only pieces in the room and it held few decorations. In fact, she only saw one picture frame in the whole room and it sat next to a wood carving on the clutter-free desk. Who was so important to him to be the only pictures in the room? Curious, she crossed to the desk and turned the frame around.

It was one of those folding frames that held two pictures. On one side was a picture of his sister, a man, and two children. Carrie assumed that was her husband and children, but it was the other side that grabbed her attention.

She stared at it trying to figure out when he could have gotten it. It was a picture of the two of them at the chapel in Vegas. A broad smile lit up his features and her head leaned against his chest. She certainly didn't look unhappy. Had she held feelings for him then? Carrie returned the frame to the desk and picked up the wood carving. It was beautiful and eerie. Whoever carved it had created a woman's face. A very familiar woman's face. She traced the curve of the face, and her eyes widened. Was that her face staring back at her? She replaced the carving and backed out of the room closing the door behind her. She needed time to process what she had seen.

The next door opened to a small bathroom. Carrie

could tell a bachelor decorated it as nothing matched and the simple decor held no woman's touch. Blue towel, black shower curtain, and a plastic soap dispenser that looked like the kind you bought at general stores. Still, it was clean and clutter free like the rest of the house. He took care of his place. That she could appreciate, but the lack of necessities in the house unnerved her. What did he do for fun?

Next was a simple guest room. It held a bed, dresser, and a nightstand with a lamp. She wondered if anyone ever used it.

The last door opened to the master bedroom. Carrie paused and bit her lip. She shouldn't go in his bedroom without asking. She would hate it if someone did that to her, but she couldn't seem to stop her feet from entering.

The neatly made queen bed filled most of the room, a blue comforter spread across it. The empty nightstand on the right side led her to believe he slept on the left as that nightstand held an alarm clock, a lamp, and a Bible. His dresser was also neat. Only a small box sat on top which Carrie assumed held tie tacks or some other things. Above the dresser hung a beautiful photograph of a sun setting on a barn. The reds, oranges, and pinks in the picture came to life making Carrie feel almost as if she were there.

The only other thing in the room was a door which Carrie assumed led to the closet and maybe another bathroom. She forced herself not to open it and look. She had invaded his privacy enough.

"Did you find something you like?"

Carrie froze at the sound of his masculine voice behind her, and a heated flush clawed up her neck. She scrambled for an excuse as she turned to face him. "Sorry, I was looking for the bathroom. You forgot to give me the complete tour earlier."

His eyebrow arched in a sexy, teasing expression as his hand raked across his stubbled cheek. "So I did. You'll find one through there," he nodded at the closed door, "but it's the one I use so I make no guarantees on the state of it." Cal flashed her a wink before stepping back and gesturing toward the hallway. "Or there's a guest bathroom down the hall."

"I um guess I'd prefer that one." Carrie felt tongue tied, like a schoolgirl with her first crush, and embarrassment flooded her that he had caught her snooping in his room.

"Well then, let me lead the way." Cal exited the room and Carrie meekly followed. How had he sneaked up on her?

al swallowed his laughter as Carrie ducked into the bathroom. He'd caught her snooping, but he

let her think he believed her story of getting lost. He didn't want to embarrass her any further and it gave him hope that she had gone looking. If she truly felt nothing, she wouldn't have bothered to explore his life. Besides, he had nothing to hide.

The sound of the faucet carried through the closed door, and Cal smiled. Maybe she really had wanted to clean up. If not, she was certainly playing it up. He leaned against the wall as he waited for her to open the door.

"Oh." Her startled voice matched her face as it swung open. "I didn't think you'd still be waiting out here."

"Well, I wanted to escort you to dinner, and I didn't want you getting lost again." He bit his lips to keep from laughing at the indignant look on her face.

"Ha-ha. You're quite the comedian."

"So I've been told." He flashed his most charming smile and wiggled his eyebrows at her delighted when he got a return smirk. "Shall we get some grub then?"

Carrie's response was an eye roll, but as a smile accompanied it, Cal counted it as a win in his favor.

"Stacy started the food, but I have to add the finishing touches," Cal said as they entered the kitchen. He picked up his apron and tied it around his waist before tasting the chili. "Mm, needs a little more salt." Grabbing the shaker from the counter, he poured a little more in before turning back to Carrie.

"Do you always wear that when you cook?" Her voice

was muffled behind the hand she held to her mouth and her eyes twinkled.

He looked down at his 'Kiss the Cook' apron and grinned. "It was a gift from my sister."

"And yet you still wear it." Her left eyebrow rose giving her a quizzical expression.

"Well, I wouldn't want to hurt her feelings and it keeps my shirt from getting dirty."

At that Carrie laughed out loud. "Doesn't your job as a rancher already get your shirts dirty?"

"Touché, but I promise I washed my hands before I touched any food." He smiled at her and his insides tangled. What was he going to do if she insisted on the divorce? Over the years he imagined what it would be like if she returned but having her here was way better than his imagination ever conjured.

Her face shifted, and she shrugged. "I probably won't eat much anyway. I doubt it's on my diet."

Cal raised a brow, but he wasn't offended. This wasn't the real her. In fact, it gave him hope. If she were throwing up emotional walls that meant she was feeling something for him. "Actually, I considered that. The chili is homemade, just meat and vegetables. I made cornbread too, but I'll understand if you aren't eating starches."

Her mouth fell open, but no sound came out for a minute. Then her face shifted. "How can you be sure? Didn't your sister start the chili?"

"She did, but it was my recipe, so I think I know what's in it. Do you want to grab two bowls?" He nodded at a cabinet on his right.

"Uh sure." Carrie crossed to the cabinet and pulled out two bowls. "So, your recipe, huh?"

"Yeah, it was learning to cook or starve. Turns out I'm rather good at it. This chili has won the blue ribbon at town festivals three times."

"Oh really? Well, then I look forward to judging for myself then."

"Good because it's ready."

He brought the pot to the table and dished them each up a bowl. Then he returned to the stove to retrieve the cornbread. She might not be eating any, but his mouth was watering just from the smell.

Cal set the cornbread on the table and then scooted his chair in. "I hope you're still a believer because we pray in this house over our food."

"I am," Carrie said before closing her eyes.

Cal nodded and bowed his head. "Thank you, Lord, for this day, for this food, and for bringing Carrie and me back together for however long it may be. In your name, amen."

Cal opened his eyes and tried to gauge Carrie's reaction, but she said nothing. She merely dipped her spoon into the chili, blew on it, and brought it to her mouth. He continued to glance at her as they ate. Since her arrival, he had seen two different Carries. There was the haughty one who pretended she was too good for him and this town and there was the Carrie he had taken on a tour of his land. The relaxed one who smiled and showed delight. He figured, unless she had changed drastically in six years, that she was the real Carrie and the other was an act, but he wished he knew how to get her true side to stay.

"So, I have to do a little work tomorrow morning, but would you like to see the rest of the town?"

She looked up at him briefly before dropping her eyes back to her bowl. "I don't suppose I can convince you to sign the papers tonight and let me get back to New York?"

"Nope."

"Then I'm kind of at your mercy, so let's see the town."

Cal caught the insinuation in Carrie's words. He was messing up her plans, but he couldn't lose her without a fight. The fact that she hadn't filed for divorce in all these years had to mean something. "I know you think it's a podunk town, but we have a rather interesting history."

"Can I ask you something?" Carrie's voice was direct, and her green eyes stared into his.

"Sure."

"Why do you still want me? It's been six years, so why haven't you moved on?"

Cal set his spoon down and smiled. "Before my dad

decided he wanted a simpler life, he was in the Air Force. My mom's dad was too. My grandfather introduced my father to Christ and when he was a Christian, he introduced my father to my mother - through the mail. They wrote letters back and forth for months. He proposed through the mail, she accepted through the mail, and they met face to face a week before their wedding."

"That's a sweet story," Carrie said. "How long have they been together?"

"Fifty years, and while that's amazing," he shook his head, "it's not the most amazing part."

The corners of Carrie's lips pulled into a grin. "Okay, I'll bite. What's the most amazing part?"

"My father had recently broken up with a woman he thought he would marry. When my grandfather introduced him to Christ, he prayed for God to bring his Elaine back to him." Cal paused for dramatic effect and took a drink of his tea. "My mother's name is Elaine. God answered his prayer. Just not in the way Dad figured He would."

"That is amazing, but you haven't answered my question yet."

Cal smiled at Carrie. She would keep him on his toes, but he wouldn't want it any other way. "I was getting to that. You needed the background on my parents to understand me. See, I wanted what my parents had. That real, long lasting love, but I kept not finding it. I dated before I met you, but none of them felt right. There was no feeling that 'she's the one.'

"But all that changed when I saw you. When you smiled at me with that beautiful smile, I felt something I had never felt before. I had never believed in love at first sight, but the night I saw you, I just knew. Then we spent the evening talking. I probably don't have to tell you, but you have this amazing personality. We laughed and shared stories of our past and our hopes for the future, and every time you looked at me with those green eyes, I knew I wanted to gaze into them forever.

"I should have prayed about it longer than I did, but I didn't want you to get away. The next morning when you told me you regretted the marriage, it killed me, but I took those marriage vows seriously, and I didn't feel at peace with the idea of a divorce. I prayed. No," he shook his head, "I pray every day for God's guidance on this. I trust, like my father did, that God is watching out for me and has the best planned."

Carrie sat back in her chair and her eyes studied him. "I appreciate your wanting to follow God's will, but what if His will isn't for us to stay together? I've moved on with my life, and I'm not getting the same feelings you are."

Cal matched her position, leaning back a little himself. "You seem like a knowledgeable Christian, and no doubt you've heard the phrase 'let no man separate what God has joined,' but I understand your question. You and I seem worlds apart, and you're wondering if I'll hold on to you out of spite or some misguided notion."

Carrie raised her brow but said nothing. However, her steady gaze told him he had hit the nail on the head.

"If God gives me peace about letting you go, I'll do it. I'll hate it, but I'll do it."

"Okay, as long as we're on the same page."

"We're in the same book anyway." He flashed a wide smile as he stood and gathered the dishes from the table. She took his lead and picked up the few remaining pieces handing them to him at the sink. "Will you do me a favor?" Cal plugged the sink and filled it with hot water before setting the dishes in. They could soak until Carrie left. There'd be plenty of time to wash them later.

Carrie's brow lifted, and she folded her arms across her chest. "You mean in addition to changing my plans to spend the weekend with you?"

Cal smirked as he wiped his hands on the nearby plaid towel. "Touché, but this is a small favor. I wanted to see if you would join me in my devotion tonight." He hung the towel back on the rack.

"You want to read the Bible with me?" Carrie asked.

"I do. It's something I always hoped to do with my wife, and even though you may not be here long, I would enjoy sharing that with you."

She blinked at him. "Um, okay, I guess."

Her hesitation surprised Cal. "Do you not do

devotionals with your fiancé?" Cal crossed to the living room grabbing his Bible from the coffee table as he did.

Carrie's eyes shifted to the side. "Well, we haven't yet, but I'm sure we will when we marry. We're both busy professionals, but he attends church with me." She pushed her nose up in the air as if that settled the discussion.

"If you're too busy now, how are you going to make the time when you're married?" He meant it as an innocent question, but Carrie bristled as if he'd attacked her.

"We just will. I'll make sure it's a priority." Her defensive tone told Cal he had hit a nerve, and he backed off. He wanted to win her over not push her away.

"I hope you do." He sat on the edge of the couch. "I think it's the most important time a couple can spend together. I'm in Isaiah. Join me?" Cal patted the couch beside him.

Carrie hesitated a moment but sat down next to him. Far enough away, he noticed, that she didn't have to touch him. Cal smiled to himself as he flipped the pages to the right chapter. Baby steps, he reminded himself. He would need to take baby steps to win her over.

arrie entered the hotel room in a fog of confusion that night. Dinner with Cal had been

amazing. Even though she knew he needed to cook to eat, she couldn't remember the last time a man had cooked for her. Philippe always took her out to restaurants or ordered food in. While that was nice, she wondered if he would ever cook for her. With her money, she could hire a cook - he could as well - but there was something about a man cooking a meal for her that warmed her heart. Perhaps it stemmed back to memories of her father.

He had worked several years on Wall Street and when she was growing up, she rarely saw him. He left before she woke in the morning and arrived home after she'd gone to bed for the night most nights, but when he finally made his million, well several of them actually, he quit Wall Street and lived off the amazing investments he had made until the cancer got him. Carrie had been eight or ten when that happened, and she had loved waking to the smell of bacon in the skillet or pancakes on the grill.

Then there was the devotional. While Philippe attended church with her, he had never offered to read a devotional with her, but she had also never asked. Would he if she asked? Carrie wasn't sure, but she had enjoyed the time with Cal. Listening to his deep, velvety voice was enjoyable in and of itself, but discussing the reading with him was even better. He was much more knowledgeable than Carrie was, and she found herself hanging on his every word.

The whole experience left her confused to say the

least, and she needed to talk to Gwen about it. Carrie was glad Gwen's number was on speed dial because she wasn't sure she would have been able to recall the number in her current condition.

The phone rang twice before Gwen answered. "How did it go?"

"It was interesting." Carrie sat on the bed, her mind a jumble of emotions. "Cal took me riding."

"Riding?" Gwen's voice held the same disbelief Carrie had felt. "Riding what? Horses?"

Carrie chuckled. "Yeah. I think he thought putting me on a horse and showing me his land would just magically change my mind about staying married to him. He even asked if I had to be in New York to design. Can you believe that? Like who would I design for out here?" Carrie hated the tone of her voice, but she was so confused.

She had come here expecting a quick conversation, maybe even a laugh as they traversed memory lane, and then departing and returning to her life with a signature on the papers. What she hadn't expected was this. This jumble of feelings colliding within her. She hadn't expected Cal to be so handsome or her heart to flip whenever he got near her. She hadn't expected the story he told her at dinner or to be questioning her engagement, her job, or her life. But she was.

"Did you tell him how you felt?" Gwen asked.

Carrie snorted. "Yeah, and he said God could find a way to make it all work. I mean I believe in God, but that just sounds like Cal using God as an excuse to make me stay."

Gwen was silent on the other line. Carrie could tell there was something was on her mind, but she didn't dare ask. At least not right now. She was still battling her own thoughts, and she didn't need Gwen's confusing her even more.

"Then he made me dinner."

"He made you dinner?" Surprise laced Gwen's voice.

"Yeah, nothing big. It was chili, but it was superb." Carrie traced the flower pattern on the bedspread with her finger.

"I'd say it's something. He didn't have to cook for you."

"Well, he had to eat. Anyway, he wants to show me the town tomorrow, so we'll see how that goes."

"Okay, I'll keep praying for you over here. Just remember to be open to God's words."

"I'll try. I just wish He would speak a little louder."

Carrie hung up the phone and plugged it into her charger. Then she wandered into the bathroom to brush her teeth and get ready for bed. She stared at her reflection in the mirror as she brushed her teeth. Open to God's words. She thought she was open to His words, but He didn't seem to be speaking into her ear. Carrie wished, as she had often in the past, that God would yell in her ear. She wanted to be sure she was doing the right thing.

With a sigh, she rinsed her mouth, brushed her hair, and then flicked the bathroom light off. As she changed into her pajamas, she sent up a silent prayer for wisdom.

CHAPTER 8

*C*arrie woke to the beeping alarm of her cell phone the next morning. She turned it off and, out of habit, checked her messages for one from Philippe, but the mailbox icon on her phone remained empty. That was odd. He almost always texted her before going to work. Perhaps he had been working late and simply slept in this morning. But it was Saturday, and he usually worked on Saturdays at least in the morning. He should be getting ready for work, or with the time difference already be at work. Maybe he was with clients and had just turned his phone off.

Figuring that was why he hadn't answered, Carrie kicked off the covers and padded to the bathroom to shower. Cal had said he would pick her up late morning, whatever time that was, and she wanted to eat before he arrived. The warm water erased the last lingering bit of sleep and Carrie stepped out of the shower feeling refreshed and ready to take on the day. And Cal. She needed to keep her feelings in check today and not get sucked into his dreamy eyes and sweet smile.

Carrie wiped the fog off the mirror and leaned in to regard her appearance. Was it her imagination or did her skin look better than normal? She didn't have bad skin, but she always needed to add some tinted base to her face in New York to give her skin a little color, but she didn't need it today. Her skin shone, and her eyes sparkled back at her. Was it the Texas weather or was it Cal?

Irritated that thoughts of Cal kept invading her mind, she quickly brushed her hair and teeth before flicking off the light and heading to the closet to get dressed.

Her options were limited as she had brought little with her, but not knowing what Cal had in store for her, Carrie changed into the most functional outfit she had - a pair of flared pants and matching shirt she designed last summer. If she ended up staying much longer, she would have to see about finding a laundromat or a store.

The tempting aroma of bacon drifted in the air as Carrie neared the kitchen, and her stomach rumbled. She hadn't thought she was hungry, but her stomach begged to differ. Carrie entered the homey dining room and grabbed a seat by the window. Only a few other tables filled the room and currently she was the only diner. Dixie, however, appeared a moment later.

"Well, good morning, Carrie. Did you sleep okay?"

"I did, thank you." Surprisingly, the bed had been quite comfortable. Not her own bed by any means but more comfortable than many hotel beds she had stayed in.

Dixie smiled and clasped her hands together. "Wonderful, well I've made eggs and bacon and pancakes. What would you like?"

The tiny spontaneous part of Carrie almost said pancakes - one of her guilty pleasures - but she had been low carb for weeks. "Mm, the bacon smells delicious, so I think I'll take the eggs and bacon."

"Coming right up. Help yourself to coffee or juice at the counter there." Dixie pointed to a little table on the other side of the room. It held a coffee carafe, a pitcher of orange juice, a basket of creamer and cups and mugs.

"Thank you." Carrie smiled up at the woman as she stood. "I will certainly partake in a little of that."

Dixie smiled back and nodded before disappearing through a swinging door near the back of the room. Carrie continued to the table and picked up a ceramic mug. Each one held a different saying or picture, and the one she held currently had the words "Chocolate solves everything" emblazoned across it. Carrie smiled at the apt description of her - interesting that she would choose that mug. She poured a little cream and sugar into the mug and then filled the rest with coffee enjoying the way the dark liquid swirled with the cream to create a satisfying tan color. She had never been able to drink her coffee black.

Dixie reached the table at the same time Carrie was returning. "Bacon and eggs," she said placing the plate down.

"Thank you." Carrie set her mug down and then pulled the chair out to sit down again.

"Can I ask you something?" Dixie asked.

"Uh, sure, I guess." Carrie had no idea what she could want to ask a perfect stranger.

Dixie pulled out the opposite chair and sat down. Then she leaned forward as if sharing a juicy secret. "Where did you get your outfit? It's so beautiful and stylish."

Carrie blinked, caught off guard by the question. "I made it. I'm a designer."

Dixie's eyes grew wide. "You made it?"

"Yeah, that's kind of what I do." Carrie took a sip of the coffee and appraised Dixie. Though older, it was clear the woman took care of herself, but her style did leave a lot to be desired. Today, she wore a basic pair of black pants, a solid red shirt, and a black-and-white checkered vest.

Dixie folded her hands and leaned her chin upon them. "I wish we had clothes like that in our general store, but supplies are limited. Of course, you can order online, but then there's the hassle of returns if it doesn't fit."

"That is a hassle." Carrie had always loved designing but one reason she stuck with it was for that very reason. She wanted to help women look their best and outfits online rarely fit correctly unless you had the perfect body type. "Maybe one day a designer will move to town." She had hoped to pray before eating, but as it appeared Dixie was in no hurry to leave, Carrie threw up a silent thank you and took a bite of the eggs.

"Yes, maybe," Dixie's eyes twinkled, "So, you and Cal-"

"Are just friends," Carrie finished before Dixie probed any further. She should have known that question would come up.

Dixie's face fell in a portrait of disappointment. "Oh, that's too bad. He's such a nice guy, but he won't date anyone around here though many have tried. Rumor is that he's pining for a woman from his past."

"Sorry, I wouldn't know," Carrie said with a shrug, careful to keep her face stoic.

"Well, I guess I'll keep praying she comes back then. I was sure hoping with the way he looks at you that he had finally moved on. He will be an amazing husband to some woman one day." Dixie pushed back her chair and stood up.

"I'm sure he will." Dixie nodded before returning to

the kitchen and allowing Carrie to return to her breakfast. Her thoughts no longer remained on the eggs and bacon though. They now firmly lingered on Cal. *Did* he really gaze at her differently? More importantly, did it matter to her? Her life was back in New York with Philippe, so she shouldn't care how Cal looked at her, but if she were honest with herself, she did.

❀

*C*al pulled up in front of the inn and took a deep breath. He wasn't sure how much longer he had, but he imagined Carrie wouldn't stick around much longer. Today would be important, and he needed everything to be perfect. He stepped out of the truck and ran a hand down his green plaid shirt. It was his favorite and Ginny often made it a point to tell him how handsome he looked in it more than once. Cal hoped Carrie might feel the same.

He opened the door of the inn and smiled at the remaining smell of breakfast. Dixie was a good cook, but he hoped to convince Carrie to join him for breakfast tomorrow. He made a mean skillet.

"Morning, Cal," Dixie said as she entered the foyer. "Carrie's in the dining room."

"Thank you." Cal nodded. "I figured that's where I'd find her. Breakfast sure smells delicious."

"You want me to grab you some bacon?"

Cal shook his head. "No, I already ate, and I'm planning to show Carrie the town today, but perhaps we'll come back for dinner."

Dixie's eyes lit up. "Oh, you should. Dan and I were planning a little impromptu party with music and dancing, maybe a movie."

"Oh, yeah, what's the occasion?" Cal racked his brain, but he couldn't place any nearby holiday. Easter had just passed, and Cinco de Mayo remained over a week away.

Dixie's wide eyes shifted to the left. "Oh, um, it's the anniversary of the inn. Been open for over one hundred years this year." Dixie's parents had run the inn before her and evidently her parents had run it before them. Cal knew Dixie's family was one of the first residents, but he'd had no idea they had been in business that long.

"Well, that's amazing, but why aren't we making a bigger deal of it? The whole town should be in on something like that." The festivals were one thing Cal loved about a small town. There was a festival nearly every month of the year, but the apple festival and the cowboy roundup were their two biggest - both of which happened in the summer months.

"I thought it would be nice to have a smaller affair on the actual day and then we can plan something bigger for next month. You'll come, won't you?"

"Sure." Cal shrugged. He wanted to show Carrie the

town, but what better way to show her the small-town lure but a party. "Wouldn't miss it for the world."

"Great, well, I have to get planning, I mean, decorating and cooking. We'll start at 6pm. See you then." And then without another word, Dixie disappeared into the kitchen.

Cal shook his head and continued into the dining room to find Carrie. She sat at a table by the window sipping on a mug. As her eyes were focused out the window, he took a moment to study her. Her green pantsuit made the red and gold in her hair stand out even more than usual. He wondered if she had any idea how beautiful she was.

As if she sensed his eyes, Carrie turned his direction. A slight smile stole across her lips as Cal crossed the room to her. "Hey, Carrie."

"Hey Cal. You look nice."

"As do you. Are you ready?"

She glanced into her mug and sighed. "Yep, coffee's gone, so I guess I am."

"Big coffee fan, huh?" he asked. He hadn't taken her for a caffeine junkie.

"Not really. I like to have one maybe two cups a day but any more than that makes my stomach feel weird." She stood and pushed her chair in. "If I need something warm after that, I usually opt for green tea."

Cal didn't tell her he generally drank an entire pot by

himself, but he guessed he was also up much earlier than she was.

"Should I take the dishes somewhere?" Carrie asked uncertainly as she looked around.

"No, Dixie will take care of them. Part of the guest experience."

"All right, if you're sure," she said.

Cal wanted to hold out his hand, but he wasn't sure she would take it and he didn't want to make her uncomfortable. She smiled as he held the door open for her.

"We're going to walk?" Carrie asked as he turned away from the truck.

"Are you opposed to a little exercise?"

"No, it's just… it looks like it's about to rain." Her nose wrinkled as she stared up at the dark sky, but Cal wasn't sure if it was from disgust or fear.

The clouds looked a little menacing, but a little rain never hurt anyone. "Are you afraid of rain?" He bit the inside of his lip to keep from laughing out loud at her. The woman he married six years ago would have danced in a fountain with him if he'd asked her, but now she appeared hesitant. Again, he wondered what had made her change so drastically.

Her eyes narrowed, and he knew he had pushed a button. "No, I'm not afraid of the rain." She tossed him a haughty glare. "Come on."

This time Cal did chuckle. Here was a glimpse of the girl from six years ago - feisty and unwilling to appear weak.

"Well, where do we start?" she asked as she scanned the area.

"Right here. I just found out today that the inn is one of the oldest buildings in town. Evidently, they've been open over one hundred years."

Her eyebrow formed a pointed arch. "You just found out today?"

Cal shrugged. "So, I'm not a town history buff, but Dixie said they are having a small party tonight to celebrate. Anyway, the post office over there was another of the first buildings in Soda Spurs."

"Why is it named Soda Spurs?" Carrie asked as they walked up the street.

Cal blinked at her. He had never looked up why the town was named what it was. He simply accepted it. "You got me there," he said with another shrug. "I have no idea."

"If you're going to be a tour guide and tell people the town has an interesting history, you really should learn a few of its facts." Her words could have sounded harsh, but her teasing tone and impish smile softened them.

"I've missed this side of you." Cal sneaked a sideways glance at her. "This spunky personality is the one I fell in love with. Why have you been hiding her?"

"I haven't been hiding anything." There was a defensive hint in her words, and her nose lifted into the air. "She comes out back home."

"Does she?" Cal didn't believe her. Something had changed her over the last six years.

"Why won't you sign the papers?" Carrie asked abruptly switching the topic.

"We exchanged vows, Carrie. That means something to me. Doesn't it to you?"

"We rushed into it, Cal. That doesn't mean we have to force it to work."

He shook his head. How would he get her to understand? "We may have rushed into it, Carrie, but that doesn't make it wrong. I've asked God often if I should let you go, and He's never told me yes."

Carrie looked as if she wanted to argue more, but before she could, a large drop of rain smacked her nose. A yelp escaped her lips and her hand swiped the bridge of her nose. "I think we better head back."

"It's just a drop of rain. You're not going to melt." But before the sentence completely left his mouth, the dark skies opened up and poured down buckets of rain. Within seconds, Carrie's red hair was plastered to her face, and her eyes were wide with shock.

She looked as if she was about to bolt back to the inn, but Cal seized the moment and her hand. He had to make her remember. "Come on."

"Cal, we'll catch pneumonia," she said.

He flashed her his best grin and squeezed her hand. "First, that's an old wives' tale, and second, so what? We can be sick together." That thought held great appeal for him. He wouldn't mind caring for Carrie while she snuggled under a blanket. "Have a little fun, Carrie."

Her eyes narrowed to thin slits. She might have looked fierce if it weren't for the black trails of mascara snaking down her cheeks. "I have fun."

"Then prove it. Come run in the rain with me." He let go of her hand and took off running for the elementary school a block away, hoping he had goaded her enough that she would follow. It didn't take long before he heard her footsteps behind him, but he'd had a head start and his legs were longer, so he still reached the school first. He touched the brick wall before turning to face her.

"You cheated," she said with labored breath when she reached him. Her finger reached out to poke him in the chest and he grabbed it and pulled her closer to him.

"I gave you a chance." Cal had been a track star in high school. He could have easily outdistanced her had he wanted to, but this wasn't about winning. It was about getting her to relax and drop the emotional wall she had built some time since he'd last seen her.

Their gazes locked, and her lips parted. Cal took that as his sign and leaned forward. How perfect would a kiss in the pouring rain be? Movie perfect, that was how perfect. Time seemed to slow down as he inched closer, and the heat between them grew. Her lips were inches from his when he closed his eyes. The beating of his heart sped up in anticipation of the moment he had only dreamed of for years, but when he reached the place he thought her lips would be, there was nothing but air.

Then her hand escaped his grasp and pushed against his chest. "Cal, I can't. Not while I'm engaged to someone else."

Cal wanted to protest, to remind her that they were married, but he didn't want to push her back into her shell. And she had said not while she was engaged to someone else which gave him hope that she was reconsidering their divorce. He could wait a little longer if it meant he could be with her forever.

"You're right. I'm sorry. I got caught up in the moment."

"Me too." Her voice was soft as her eyes sought his. They still brimmed with a hunger, and it was clear she was fighting the urge to kiss him as well.

Though desire still clouded his vision, he would respect her words. "We could have more moments like these," Cal said. His hand twitched at his side. He wanted so badly to touch her face, to feel her cheek in his hand.

Carrie's eyes slid to the side and Cal wondered if he had stepped too far. He wished he could rewind time and take the words back.

"This was dumb," Carrie began, and Cal's heart dropped, but then her lips curled into a small smile, "we should have run toward the inn. Now, we just have farther to walk back in the rain."

Though she tried for a teasing tone again, he could hear the difference in her voice. The moment was gone, and all Cal could do was hope he would have another chance.

CHAPTER 9

When they reached the truck, Cal opened the door for her and she slid in feeling a little like a drowned rat. He entered the other side a moment later and started the truck, turning on the heater to warm them up and dry them off a little.

"Okay, that was more than a little rain," he said with a smile, "but I can give you most of the rest of the tour from here anyway. Over there is the town hall and Marnie's, a sit down but casual eatery." He shifted in his seat to point out her window. "Down that street is the flower shop, the general store, and Ernesto's, a more upscale restaurant, though I'm confident it's nothing like you have in New York."

"Can we stop at the general store?" Carrie asked. She wasn't sure why but she wanted to see what they offered.

Dixie's comments were still rattling around in her brain, and she hated that such a nice woman couldn't get the kind of clothes she wanted.

"Uh sure," Cal said putting the truck in drive, "Any particular reason why?"

"I want to see their clothing section."

His lips twitched at the corners. "Feeling the desire to dress a little more casually?"

"Something like that."

The general store was much smaller than Carrie had expected, about double the size of her apartment back home. They made a mad dash for the inside as the rain still poured down.

"Perhaps we should get an umbrella," Carrie said with a laugh as she shook the water out of her hair.

"Hey, watch where you're flinging that mane." Cal held up his hands and turned away from her.

"Oh, sorry, did that get you wet?" Carrie grinned and shook her hands at him sending a few more droplets his way.

"What's going on here?" A deep voice asked from behind her. Carrie's smile faded, and she lowered her hands.

Cal's smile, on the other hand, deepened. "Sorry, Jim. It's a little wet outside. I guess we got a little carried away. If you'll point me toward a towel, I'll clean it up for you."

"Nah, I'll get one of the employees to clean it up, but you can introduce me to your friend."

Carrie turned around to face the man and stuck out her hand. "I'm Carrie Bliss." As she regarded him, she had the distinct feeling she had seen him before though she couldn't place where.

Jim took her hand but flashed wide eyes Cal's direction as if for confirmation. Cal nodded. "Jim, Carrie. Carrie this is my brother-in-law, Jim."

Brother-in-law. Now, Carrie understood why he seemed familiar. This must be Stacy's husband and she had recognized him from the picture on Cal's desk. "Nice to meet you, Jim. I'm sorry about the water. It was my fault."

"Ah, well in that case, I'm certain Cal deserved it," Jim said with a smile.

"Hey," Cal protested but his smile told Carrie that he knew Jim was teasing him.

"Anyway, don't worry about it. I'll get one of the guys to lay out some extra mats. I'm positive you two won't be the last wet customers we have today."

"Thanks, Jim. See you guys at church tomorrow?"

"You bet. It was nice to meet you Carrie." Though he said the words to her, Carrie didn't miss the expression he flashed Cal's direction. He must know who she was.

"So, clothing section?" Cal asked as Jim walked away.

Carrie nodded and followed him to the right. The

general store was set up much like a Walmart only on a much smaller scale. Groceries were to the left and everything else was to the right. The whole clothing department was about the size of Carrie's bedroom, and the selection was dismal to say the least. Two racks of dresses in sizes six to fourteen, two racks of shirts, and one rack each of pants and skirts. Nearly everything was either monochromatic or plaid flannel and all of it lacked imagination.

"Are you looking for something in particular?" Cal asked as Carrie flicked through the offerings.

"No, I just wanted to see the offerings." It was clear now why Dixie wished more was available. It would be hard to have an individual style with what was here. She wondered how profitable a shop would be out here? Maybe she could hire someone to run a small branch. Surely rent wouldn't be expensive in such a small town, but would it make enough to be profitable?

Carrie shook her head. She was getting ahead of herself. The first thing she needed to do was find out what kind of clothing Dixie wanted and if she had an idea on what might sell. Then she could figure out the cost and see if what the people could afford would be profitable to her.

"You're not going to buy anything?" Cal asked.

A laugh escaped Carrie's mouth before she registered how rude it must sound. She composed herself and thought about her words carefully. "Uh, not yet. Nothing here is really my style, but I do want an umbrella. Plus, I rather think I owe your brother-in-law."

"You don't, but all right, let's get you an umbrella." Cal led the way to a small sporting good section and Carrie chose a simple black one.

After paying, they headed back to the truck, but the rain had stopped, and Carrie had no need to open the umbrella. The air had cooled though, and she found herself wishing she had brought a coat.

"I'd be happy to finish the tour, but do you mind if we stop by the ranch, so I can check on Dexter and the herd?"

"Sure." Carrie shrugged. "I'm at your mercy today."

Cal pulled into the ranch and Carrie opened her door and stepped out. Involuntarily, a shiver raced down her spine. The air had certainly cooled with the rain.

Cal's eyes filled with concern, and he closed the space between them. "Are you cold? Come inside with me, and I'll get you a jacket."

"No, I'm fine," Carrie protested, but even as she did, another gust of wind hit her, and she shook again.

"You are not." His hands twitched at his side causing her to wonder if he was fighting the urge to wrap them around her. "Look, it's going to take a bit for me to check on the herd, and I don't want you freezing. Please, just humor me?"

His emerald eyes pleaded with her, and a flicker of déjà vu surfaced in Carrie's mind.

"I'm not drunk, Cal," Carrie said as she wrapped her arms around his neck. *She knew this was crazy, but she'd felt a connection from the first moment he approached her on the dance floor. The gaze he sent her way made her feel something she had never felt before, something she hadn't even known she was even craving, and she didn't want to let go.*

He tucked a strand of hair behind her ear, and his hand traced a trail down her face to cup her chin. "You say that now, but I want you to be certain. This is marriage we're talking about, so please just humor me and drink the coffee?"

"If it will make you feel better," she said with a wink. *She dropped one arm to the table and picked up the mug of tan liquid. She took a sip and then downed the rest of the coffee. He watched her with a bemused smile and twinkling eyes. When she was finished, she placed the mug back on the counter and turned to him with a challenging stare. "Done, now can we go get married?"*

Oh gracious. She hadn't been drunk. She had felt something for him then. No wonder he had been so shocked when she performed a one eighty the next morning.

"Are you okay?"

This time his hand did touch her arm, and Carrie started at the heat that seared up her arm. The image from the past shattered in her mind. "Yeah, fine, I'll take you up on that coat."

"Good, come on."

Carrie followed Cal into the house expecting him to turn down the hallway to the bedrooms, but he stopped just inside the door and pulled a leather jacket off the coat tree.

A masculine scent washed over her as she took the jacket from him and another memory flooded her mind. The woodsy cologne rising from the leather was the same one that had filled her nose the night they married.

"Are you two sure you want to get married?" The minister, an Elvis impersonator in a sparkly white jumpsuit, regarded them as he posed the question.

Carrie looked around the wedding chapel. She wasn't certain getting married in an Elvis chapel had been her dream but marrying Cal would be worth it. "We're sure," Carrie said as she took Cal's hands.

He squeezed them and flashed a return smile. "Never been surer of anything in my life."

"All right, well then let's get this hunk a hunk of burning love legal." He took the marriage certificate from Cal and scanned over the names. "Dearly beloved," he began in an Elvis drawl. "We are gathered here today to join this man and this woman in holy matrimony."

"You coming?"

"Huh?" Carrie blinked the memory away and focused on Cal who stood staring at her. He had on another leather jacket, black to match his hat.

"I asked if you wanted to come. You could ride on the back of Ginger with me."

"Um, okay all right." Carrie wasn't positive she should be getting up on a horse behind Cal. She was even less sure she should wrap her arms around him and breathe in his scent, but the words were already out, and her feet carried her his direction anyway.

Cal led the way outside and to the barn. Carrie watched as he saddled up his horse and then led her out of the barn. He swung up first and then held his hand out to her. "Just put your foot in the stirrup like last time, and I'll help pull you up."

"Okay." Carrie followed his directions and before she knew it, she was up and behind him. Her arms wrapped around his waist and she held on for dear life as he urged the horse to speed up. Even through her fear, the heat radiating off Cal reached Carrie. Her heart thudded in her chest at being so close to him and inhaling the woodsy scent coming off him. For the first time since she'd arrived, Carrie knew that if she didn't leave soon, she might never want to go, and it terrified her.

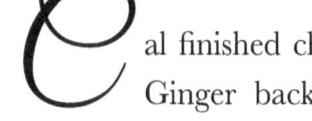al finished checking on the herd and then urged Ginger back to the house. He didn't want to

return as he was relishing the presence of Carrie's body pressed against his back, but he had promised to show her the rest of the town, and the weather had him a little worried. The air had shifted again, and the dark clouds looked as though they might pour more rain down any moment.

"Why don't you head inside while I take care of Ginger?" Cal suggested. Carrie's face was flushed though whether it was from the cold or the proximity they had shared, he wasn't sure. He hoped it was the latter.

"Are you sure?" she asked. Her eyes found his for a moment before glancing away, but in that small moment, he read the desire and confusion in her gaze.

"Yeah, I'm sure. Make yourself at home. I'll just be a minute." He smiled as he walked Ginger to the barn. Carrie was remembering. He was almost sure of it. Twice he had caught her staring off into space. If he could get her to remember that night - well, he had to. It would change everything.

He removed the saddle and brushed Ginger down quickly before returning to the house. He found Carrie staring at the photo above the fireplace.

"Ready?" he asked as he entered.

She turned to him, an unreadable expression on her face. "Do you have a television?"

"What?" He hadn't been expecting that question.

"A television. You know. TV." She turned back toward

the fireplace. "The black box you watch entertainment on."

Cal's lips twitched. "I am aware of what a TV is. Yes, there's one in my bedroom though I don't watch it much. Why do you ask?"

Carrie's thin shoulders rose slightly and fell back down. "Everyone in my circle has multiple TVs. I found it odd that you didn't have one in here."

Would that be a deal breaker for her or was she comparing him to the men in her life? "I've never been much for TV. Too many other things to occupy my time."

She turned back to him, her forehead wrinkled in confusion. "In this town?"

"There's so much to a small town. There's community and nearly every month we have a festival. Almost everyone comes out and pitches in with food or decorations or music. I bet you don't even know your neighbors' names, am I right?"

Carrie sucked in a breath, opened her mouth as if to answer, and then sighed. "Guilty. I can recall the doorman's name and that's about it."

"See here everyone knows everyone else in town. There's an army to help if you're sick or down on your luck. People pray for you, say hello in the grocery store. You learn about your neighbors and friends, so yeah there are too many other things to do besides watch other people live on a black box."

Carrie held his gaze for a minute as if taking in his words. "Where did this picture come from?" She pointed to the landscape shot above the fireplace.

"Stacy took it."

Her eyes widened. "Stacy took it?"

Cal shrugged. "Yeah, she always had a photo bug growing up. I remember when she first got a camera. I think she was six. Most girls that age wanted dolls or stuffed animals, but not Stacy. She wanted a camera, and she was really careful with it. It took her awhile, but by the next Christmas, she was taking amazing pictures. She learned how to develop her own in high school."

"Why didn't she become a photographer then? She's talented."

"She met Jim and wanted to raise a family. Now she takes pictures in her free time kind of like my whittling."

"You whittle?" Her eyes shifted to the side as if puzzle pieces were falling into place.

"I do." He said the words slowly wondering if she would elaborate on why she was asking. "Ranching can be a little lonely in the evenings without someone to share them with. I whittle to pass the time."

Her eyes caught his, and his breath stilled. The desire to kiss her flooded through his veins creating a pounding sensation in his head. Electricity crackled in the air, and he leaned forward.

"It's beautiful, the picture I mean." Her voice was soft, but she had pulled back. The moment was broken.

"Thank you." Cal swallowed his disappointment and motioned to the kitchen. "Shall we get some lunch? I don't want to eat anything too big because if I know Dixie, she'll have a feast planned."

Carrie nodded and followed him into the kitchen.

CHAPTER 10

When the sandwiches were gone, and the paper plates thrown away, Cal held out his hand to Carrie. "Can I show you something?"

She nodded and took his hand, but as he led her down the hallway to the guest room, she protested, "Cal, what are you doing?"

"Just wait." The simple guest room didn't contain much, but it held one large secret. He opened the door to the closet and stepped back. Inside he had installed a few shelves and they were lined with his carvings.

She gasped as she stepped forward. Her hand touched a few of the carvings, delicately as if she were afraid they would crumble under her fingers. "Cal, these are beautiful. Why do you keep them hidden?"

"They're nothing special, only a hobby."

She turned to face him, her beautiful green eyes shining with intensity. "These are not nothing, Cal Roper. They are amazing, and people would pay big money for these."

This was the moment. He felt it. "What changed you, Carrie?" He held his breath hoping she would answer and he hadn't misread her.

Her eyes held his, bored into his soul as if searching his intentions. Then she sighed. "My dad got sick. Shortly after I graduated from college."

Cal could tell there was more to this story, so he crossed to the bed and sat down. Then he patted the space next to him. Carrie hesitated but finally joined him.

"I told you in Vegas I wanted to be a designer. When I graduated, my dad gave me money to start my boutique, but then he was diagnosed with cancer. My mom was a stay at home mother, and my dad's money was consumed pretty quickly with the treatments. I tried to sell the boutique to help out, but he wouldn't let me. He died a few months later, and I swore that I would be successful to make my dad proud."

Cal placed his hand on Carrie's. "Carrie, I'm sure your dad is proud of you. You are an amazing woman." His other hand stroked her face, and she leaned into it. Oh, how Cal wanted to kiss her. He wanted to hold her in his arms and kiss all the hurt and pain away. It made sense now, this drastic change from the carefree girl he had married to the focused woman in front of him now.

As if Carrie sensed his desire, she pulled away from his touch and stood up. "Anyway, enough of my past. We should head back to the inn. Maybe we can help Dixie out."

Disappointment flooded Cal, but he nodded and stood. He would continue trying. Whatever it took, he would keep trying.

❦

*T*he ride back into town was quiet, but Cal pointed out a few of the more memorable places on the outskirts of town, like Norma's and Fannie's place before continuing to the inn. Carrie hoped Dixie would need some help. She needed a break from Cal and his magnetism.

She'd almost kissed him back there when he'd asked about her father. The moment had been perfect with his hand on her cheek, but then she'd thought of Philippe. Philippe had never inquired about her father. Of course, to be fair Philippe hadn't known her before her father passed away, but he had never asked about any of her family.

A touch on her elbow brought her back to the present. "We're here. You ready?"

"Yeah." Carrie tucked her hair behind her ears and pulled back her shoulders. She could do this. She could get through the evening without thinking about kissing Cal.

Inside, the inn was a flurry of activity. Carrie almost didn't even recognize the place. The furniture in the living room had been pushed to the walls to open up the floor and beautiful flower arrangements filled the room.

"I can see Rose has been here," Cal said with a slight chuckle as he scanned the room.

"Who's Rose?"

"She runs the local flower shop. Ironic, right?"

Carrie grinned at him. "Um, that's not really irony, but it is interesting."

Tiny creases erupted at the top of Cal's nose. "What's irony then?"

"Well, there's three types but the one you mean is situational irony. That's when an event is contrary to what one expects and is often amusing because of it."

The creases deepened. "And that's not the same thing as Rose running the flower shop?"

"Not quite." Carrie smiled and swatted his arm playfully. "Let's go see if Dixie needs any more help."

They found Dixie in the kitchen surrounded by piles of goodies. "Oh good," she said when she spotted them, "I'm not sure where the rest of my helpers went. Can you two bring all this to the dining room? We're going to set it up on tables and let guests grab what they want."

"Sure, Dixie, we'd be happy to." Cal picked up a few of the trays and Carrie followed suit. They passed through the swinging door and into the dining room where a woman was hanging a sign that read 'Happy 100 Years!'

"Hey, Rose," Cal said as he placed a tray down on one of the tables. "The living room looks great."

"Thanks." She finished attaching the last corner of the sign and turned to them. "Next time, I hope Dixie gives me more notice though. I had to freehand the sign." She glanced at Carrie. "I don't think we've met. I'm Rose."

"Carrie." Carrie shook her hand. "I'm a friend of Cal's."

Rose shot Cal a look but to Carrie she said, "Nice to meet you. Why don't you two go into the living room? I can help Dixie finish in here."

"No one was in the living room," Cal began but the sound of music cut him off. "I stand corrected. Apparently, there is now. Shall we, Carrie?"

"Sure." Carrie followed him out of the dining room and back toward the living room where an older couple now danced slowly around the floor. Other guests?

"I'd love to fill your dance card. What do you say?" Cal's eyes sparkled in the light, and tiny gold flecks appeared that reminded Carrie of fireflies though it had been ages since she had seen one.

Fireflies rarely appeared in New York, but Carrie remembered one summer when her parents took her camping. Out in the dark, they had zipped back and forth amazing and delighting her with their color.

Carrie blinked to shake the pull of Cal's gaze. She should say no. It probably wasn't right for her to be dancing with Cal, especially with the crazy feelings that kept popping up randomly - feelings that perhaps she should be with Cal instead of Philippe. But they were simply that, crazy, impetuous feelings that meant nothing. Those feelings had gotten her married to a stranger in the first place, and she wasn't that spur-of-the-moment impetuous girl any more.

"I doubt it is in danger of filling up," Carrie said with a teasing smile as she glanced around the room, "but sure."

Cal chuckled, and Carrie smiled at the sound. It was rich and velvety and relaxed, not at all like Philippe's laugh which always sounded tight and forced to Carrie. She shook her head as Cal took her hand and led her to the middle of the floor. She had no business comparing Philippe to Cal. Cal was her past and Philippe was her future, wasn't he?

As his arms wound around her waist, her thoughts drifted back to Gwen's wedding. Philippe wouldn't even dance with her there, but Cal spun her around the small wooden floor as if there was no place he'd rather be. Her mind flashed back even further, and she remembered dancing in Cal's arms in Vegas. He hadn't been self-conscious then either. He had twirled her effortlessly around that floor as well. No two left feet for him.

Her eyes glanced furtively to his face. The dark stubble on his cheeks called to her and before she could stop it, her hand was on his cheek. His feet slowed and then stopped. Time seemed to stand still as his eyes bore into hers. The gold flecks in his eyes danced, and Carrie found herself getting lost in them before her own eyes closed.

When his lips touched hers, a spark erupted in her soul. Was this what she had been missing the last six years? The reason she had run from every other man? Suddenly, the realization of what she was doing sunk in and she pushed back from Cal. "I'm sorry. We shouldn't have done that. I need…. I need some time." The pained expression on his face gave her pause, but she couldn't focus on that right now. She needed to sort through her feelings or distance herself from Cal, so she could at least think.

"Wait," Cal called out. "Can I at least pick you up for church in the morning?"

Church. Yes, that's what she needed. Church would ground her and remind her of what was important in her life. Her job, her friends, Philippe. "Sure. See you then." Then she dashed up the stairs to her room.

"*O*h, dear, I certainly wasn't expecting that reaction," Dixie said as she came over to Cal.

"I was. She's remembering what we had and she's fighting it. I just need more time." He looked at Dixie. "I'll be back in the morning to pick her up for church. Can you make sure she's ready?"

"Of course."

CHAPTER 11

*C*onfusion still clouded Carrie's mind when she came down the next morning for breakfast, and she hoped Dixie wouldn't ask what had happened. After leaving Cal, she had prayed about the situation asking for clarity, but none had come. She still felt torn in two different directions.

"Morning, Carrie," Dixie said as Carrie entered the dining room. "What would you like this morning?"

"Actually, I'll take the pancakes today." Comfort food sounded delicious this morning, and she could always work it off later.

"All right, I'll be right back."

Carrie took the opportunity to fill up a mug of coffee and pick a table. When Dixie appeared a moment later with her food, Carrie motioned for her to join her. "Dixie,

I went by the general store yesterday, and you're right. Their selection is lacking. What kind of clothes would you most like to see if there was a store here?"

Dixie's eyes twinkled. "Are you thinking of opening a shop here, Carrie Bliss?"

"Not me personally. I have to stay in New York, but I'm thinking of finding someone who might like to open a shop here."

"Oh." The disappointment was palpable in Dixie's voice, but she quickly mustered a smile. "Well, I guess clothes like you were wearing yesterday. Some flowing shirts, skirts, and pants. And more colors offered. I love plaid, but occasionally I'd like to wear something else."

Carrie chuckled at that. "Their selection didn't give a lot of options in that area to be sure. Well, I'd love to get your measurements later and send you some design sketches. Maybe while I'm working on finding someone to open the shop, I could at least send you some designs to wear to drum up anticipation."

Dixie clasped her hands together and smiled. "That would be lovely, and I would happily wear anything you sent."

"Okay, this afternoon or evening then."

As Dixie scooted back to the kitchen, Carrie took a bite of her pancake enjoying the warm buttery flavor of the fluffy flapjack. She'd have to put in an extra workout when she got home, but it would be worth it.

*C*al entered the inn unsure of what to say to Carrie. Did he bring up the kiss? Pretend it hadn't taken place? He didn't want to pretend it hadn't happened; he wanted it to happen again and often. But she was still figuring out her heart and as hard as it was, he needed to give her time to do that.

Carrie, thankfully, saved him the hassle of deciding. She stood in the doorway of the dining room, clearly finished with breakfast and waiting for him. "I hope this will do," she said indicating her pantsuit. "I hadn't planned on attending church while I was here, so I didn't bring my normal attire."

"Well, as you may have figured out, it's a farming and ranching small town community. We're pretty laid back around here, and while most people dress nicer for the Good Lord, I doubt anyone will say anything to you as a guest. Besides, what you're wearing now is nicer than a lot of people around here wear."

"Good. Now about last night. I let myself get carried away by the music and the atmosphere, but I promise it won't happen again."

Cal nodded and forced his disappointment down. "Whatever you say." He held out his arm to her, but she glanced down at it and then shook her head. Right, so she didn't want to touch him. Was that a good thing as it showed he clearly had an effect on her or a bad thing as if she'd reformed her wall and would no longer be persuaded?

They exited the inn and climbed into his truck. It wasn't far to the church, but the cool air still lingered after the recent rains. Cal didn't want to chance Carrie's catching cold or getting drenched again before they reached the small church.

As he drove, Cal hoped the Soda Spurs church would appeal to Carrie. He loved the small-town appeal, and he thought if she gave it a chance that she would as well.

The small parking lot was nearly full when they arrived, and Cal had to circle the lot to find an empty space. It wasn't usually this full, but perhaps more people had driven today instead of walking as they often did.

"Huh, I didn't realize this many people lived in this town," Carrie said as he parked the truck.

Oh no, was the snarky Carrie reappearing? He had thought she had gone away after dinner the first night, but perhaps she had just been taking a break. Cal sneaked a glance at Carrie's face, but the snide expression didn't reside there. Instead, the corners of her mouth twitched as if she was fighting the urge to smile. Was she teasing him?

"There's a lot about this town you don't know," Cal said as they approached the front door. "For example, I bet you were unaware we have a real-life billionaire in this town."

Carrie's head whipped his direction, and she turned accusatory eyes on him. "Who told you?"

"Who told me?" Cal's forehead wrinkled. That was an odd question for her to ask. "I think it's common knowledge around here."

"It is?" Her voice had a frantic edge to it which he didn't understand.

"Yeah, but even if it weren't, I'm fairly certain I'd know because Sam has worked on my truck."

"The billionaire's a mechanic?" Confusion filled Carrie's voice, and her head titled to the side as she regarded him.

"What? No, the mechanic is married to the billionaire. Look, there he is now." Cal nodded discreetly at the couple approaching on the sidewalk. "That's Brent McKasson. He used to be an actor in action movies. Played Derek McCloud."

"Why would a billionaire actor live here?" Carrie asked.

"Because he found love." Though he hadn't said the words at her, he sneaked a glance to gauge her reaction.

Her mouth opened, then closed as if she were trying to formulate the right words. Then her eyes flicked to Brent and Sam before darting back. "What does he do now?"

Cal smiled at the hint of interest he heard in her voice. Maybe if she realized some other city dweller had found a reason to stay here, she might find one as well. "He writes now. Gave up acting and pens novels. And he's happy." He added the last part just to emphasize the point a little more.

Carrie raised an eyebrow at him, but before she said anything more, Tina greeted them at the front door.

"Good morning, Cal, I see you've brought a friend."

She was fishing for answers as to who his pretty friend was, and Cal obliged her - to a point. "Hello, Tina, this is my friend, Carrie."

A twinkle flashed in Tina's eyes, and Cal expected she would want more details soon, but Tina was too poised to say anything to cause a guest discomfort. Instead, she turned her kind eyes and her motherly gaze to Carrie.

"Welcome, Carrie, I hope you'll enjoy your visit with us."

"I'm sure I will."

"Tina is the pastor's wife," Cal whispered as he led Carrie into the sanctuary.

Carrie nodded as two small figures raced toward them. "Uncle Cal," they shouted.

"Hey guys." He dropped to his knees to give his niece and nephew a hug.

"When are you going to come visit us again, Uncle Cal?" Annie asked. Her light brown hair was pulled into pigtails today, and her bright blue eyes twinkled as she grabbed his hand.

"Soon, Annie, I promise."

"How about for lunch this afternoon after church?" Stacy asked as she approached with Jim right behind her.

"Stacy, I've got company in town." Cal glanced at Carrie who seemed to be watching the scene with amusement.

"So bring her," Jim spoke up. "The more the merrier. Stacy cooks for an army anyway."

Stacy swatted his arm playfully. "I'm afraid you've got that a little backward - you eat like an army - but we would love to have you, Carrie."

"Oh, um." Carrie looked to Cal as if asking what he wanted to do. Cal wasn't sure submitting Carrie to his crazy family was such a good idea but declining the offer now would break Annie's and Tyler's hearts, and they were already staring up at him with puppy dog eyes. Plus, they were charming. Maybe they could help him convince Carrie to stay.

"Fine. We'll come to lunch, but only if Carrie agrees to let me make her breakfast tomorrow."

"Cal, I have to be getting back to New York," Carrie said.

"Well, you have to eat even if you leave tomorrow. So, what's the harm in breakfast?"

Her lips mashed together forming a tight line, and he could tell she was trying to decide how much to say in front of his family. "Fine, breakfast. It will give us a chance to talk." She flashed a pointed look his direction that told him she was ready for a decision.

Cal hoped by tomorrow morning they would be talking about starting a life together, but he would have to step up his game. He couldn't keep her here forever - he knew that.

"Okay, great," Stacy said quickly. She must have sensed the tension in the air. "We have to drop these two munchkins off, but we'll see you this afternoon, okay?"

"We'll be there." Cal watched as his sister and her family walked back toward the Sunday school room hallway before turning to Carrie. "I'm sorry. I've been promising them I would get over to visit them, and I just couldn't break their hearts again."

"You guys are close then?"

"Yeah, Stacy is my account manager and she helps out around the ranch. We've always been fairly close, but after my parents moved away, we became even closer."

"That's nice, but Cal, we do need to talk about the papers."

"Not here though," Cal said continuing into the larger room. "Right now, it's God's time."

CHAPTER 12

*C*arrie had thought she would feel uncomfortable and out of place in the little church. After all, the church she attended in New York was much larger and flashier, but she had found the church quaint and friendly. People had greeted her with smiles and warm handshakes and more names than she would ever remember. The music had been nice, the pastor a good speaker, and overall the place had seemed... genuine.

Carrie's mind had even wandered at times, conjuring up images of her attending this church with Cal on a regular basis before she shook herself back to reality. She wasn't staying. She was going home. To Philippe. The need to remind herself of that played over in her head like a broken record. Philippe was her fiancé. New York was her home. Soda Spurs was a momentary bump in her road.

"What did you think?" Cal asked as he held the truck door open for her.

"It was nice. Homey. I can understand why you like it." Though she'd never lived in one, she was beginning to perceive the charm of a small town. At her church, people said hello, perhaps they even gave you their name, but little connection continued beyond that. Here, people knew each other - the good, the bad, and the ugly. Their hellos and handshakes seemed much more genuine and Carrie couldn't deny there was an attraction to that - to friends who knew you as opposed to fellow believers who greeted you and forgot your name ten seconds later.

Carrie tried to sort out her emotions during the short ride to his sister's place, but it was like trying to untangle strands of Christmas lights that had just been thrown in a box and shook up.

On one hand, she had Philippe - handsome, wealthy, and everything she thought she had ever wanted. He attended church with her, supported her career as a designer, and he lived in New York. On paper, he appeared perfect.

And then there was Cal. Also handsome but in a more rugged way. He didn't seem to care about wealth which Carrie found refreshing. Odd but refreshing. He appeared a man of God, maybe even more than Philippe, but he was impulsive and stubborn, and he lived hundreds of miles from New York. On paper, he seemed anything but perfect, but that didn't change the way Carrie felt around him. Her heart did this funny little two step whenever he came close to her, but surely, she had the same feeling with Philippe. She was simply having trouble remembering it because being near Cal was so confusing.

Cal had asked her why she'd changed in the last six years and she supposed she had a little - losing a parent did that to you, but she hadn't thought she had changed as much as he said. But the change was clear now. The New York Carrie would never have raced through the rain like she did yesterday, and the Carrie from six years ago would have tilted her head back and danced in the puddles.

So, what had changed her? Was it simply her father's death? The need to be wealthy and make him proud had driven her daily after his death, and now that she achieved billionaire status, would she still be as driven?

Was it becoming a designer? She'd had to develop a tougher skin for sure. Design, like any "art" seemed subject to people's approvals and disapprovals, and she'd had many more people hate her designs than like her designs when she first started.

Or was it New York? She'd grown up near the city, but not in the city itself. She'd been surprised when she first moved into the city. The people there appeared more closed off, more focused on themselves. Strangers rarely said hi to one another, and it wasn't unheard of to witness a crime at least once a month if not more. Carrie always felt like she had to watch her back there, but she hadn't had that feeling here. She probably could have left the keys to the rental car in the ignition and not have had the car get stolen - something she would never do in New York.

Perhaps it was a combination of all three.

"Penny for your thoughts," Cal said peeking at her from the corner of his eye.

Carrie blew out a breath of air and shook her head. "You couldn't afford my thoughts."

"I'm good for a loan," he said taking his eyes off the road just long enough to flash her a crooked smile.

"Honestly, I'm just trying to sort out my feelings. I was so sure I knew what I wanted. Being a designer has always been my dream - I told you that and being successful in New York quickly became a part of that."

"And now?" he asked glancing at her briefly before turning his eyes back to the road.

She stared at him. How could he even ask that? She had let herself get swept up in the moment last night and kissed him. Even though she had pulled away, he had to perceive her desire. "I don't think I really have to answer that." Nor did she want to. Saying it out loud would only make it more real. "Can I ask you a question though?

How are you so confident God wants us to stay together? It's not like He speaks out loud to you."

"Perhaps not out loud, but He speaks in many other ways. Every time I pray about you, He always leads me to Psalm 27:14 which says, 'Wait for the Lord; be strong and let your heart take courage; wait for the Lord!' So, while that isn't words in the way we are used to, it's words to me."

Carrie bit her lip. She wasn't certain God had ever spoken to her the same way, but was it because He wasn't speaking or because she wasn't listening? She had long considered herself a believer but being around Cal made her realize she was going through the motions more than living for Jesus.

"Here we are," he said as he pulled up in front of a small rambler painted yellow and white.

"Oh, good. I'm starving." Carrie's stomach rumbled like a punctuation to her statement, but she didn't mind. A change of conversation would be a welcome reprieve from the intense emotions raging within her.

"Uncle Cal." The two children from earlier ran out as Cal opened his door. Their adoring looks displayed the love they held for their uncle. Carrie wondered if Philippe had any nieces and nephews. She realized she didn't know much about his family either. He had always deflected the questions when she asked.

"Hey guys." Cal opened Carrie's door before bending

down to hug his niece and nephew. "Annie, Tyler, you remember my friend Carrie from earlier right?"

"Are you going to marry her?" Annie asked as she looked at Carrie.

Carrie's eyes bulged, and she coughed as she tried to recover from her shock.

Cal smiled at Carrie before returning his attention to Annie. "Well, you never know what God has planned, but for right now, she's just a friend."

"Okay," Annie said. Carrie guessed her age to be four or five from the baby roundness still visible in her face. The boy looked a little older, perhaps seven or eight. "Dad's making hamburgers." She turned her eyes on Carrie. "Do you like hamburgers?"

"Of course, who doesn't?" Carrie usually ate her hamburgers surrounded by lettuce instead of a bun, but that was more than she needed to share with this angel.

"Cool, want to see my dolls?" Annie grabbed Carrie's hand and tugged her toward the house.

"I guess I'm going to see dolls," Carrie said with a laugh as Annie pulled her up the porch.

"Go ahead," Cal flashed a smile, "I'll come rescue you later."

Carrie followed the little girl into the house and down the hall. She tried to take in the surroundings, but all she managed to see was that Stacy was a minimalist much like Cal.

"Annie, don't go far. Lunch is almost ready," Stacy said as they passed the kitchen. "Oh, hi, Carrie."

"Hi, thanks again for inviting me."

"Come on, Carrie." The little girl tugged her a few more feet down the hall to an open door which was clearly her room if the pink walls and purple decorations were any indication. Carrie smiled as she took in the bright room. It reminded her of cotton candy at the fair.

"This is Sherri." Annie held up a cabbage patch doll dressed in a red jumper. "She has red hair just like you."

"So she does." Carrie took the doll remembering her own cabbage patch doll as a kid. She was surprised they were still being made and even more surprised they were still popular. In New York, American Girl Dolls that looked like their owners were all the rage, and while pretty, something about the simplicity of the Cabbage Patch dolls appealed to Carrie more. "She's beautiful."

"So are you," the little girl said.

"Ah, thank you." Carrie felt she should say more after the compliment, but she had no idea what.

"I think you and Uncle Cal should marry," Annie continued. "He always seems a little sad, but he looks happier now that you are here."

"Oh, well, that's good, but I live far away from here, and I'm going to have to get back home soon."

"That's too bad," Annie said as she picked up another doll. "I like playing with you."

"Annie, Carrie, lunch is ready," Stacy's voice carried from down the hall.

Relief flooded Carrie. How could a little person she didn't even know manage to say just the right things to make her uncomfortable? "I guess we better go eat."

Annie shrugged, but she put the doll down and led the way back toward the kitchen.

The rest of the family was already gathered around the table when Carrie and Annie arrived. Carrie took the seat next to Cal as Stacy helped Annie into her booster seat. A plethora of food filled the table top: hamburgers, salad, chips, and fruit. Carrie's stomach rumbled as she looked from one dish to the next.

"Shall we pray?" Jim asked.

Around the table, everyone grabbed hands and Carrie bowed her head and closed her eyes. It was odd how at home she felt. She hadn't even met Philippe's family yet, and the only other people she felt this close to were Gwen and Drew. Still, something comforting and familiar existed with Cal's family. Something she could definitely get used to.

"So, how's it going?" Stacy asked Cal as he helped her clean up after dinner.

He glanced toward the living room where Carrie worked a jigsaw puzzle with Tyler and Jim while Annie played with dolls nearby. "Not as good as I'd hoped, but better than I expected, I guess. She's relaxing, and we kissed last night. It was short, but I think she's starting to remember Vegas."

"And how long are you going to keep this up, Cal? She has a job back home I'm sure. You'll have to let her get back to it."

"I know." He picked up a plate and handed it to her at the sink. "I just keep hoping for a little more time with her."

When the table was cleared, and the dishes filled the sink, Cal joined Carrie in the living room.

"Do you do puzzles?" She grinned up at him, her eyes flashing a challenge.

"I'll have you know jigsaw puzzles are my specialty." He pulled out a chair and sat next to her.

"I thought ranching was your specialty."

"I have many talents." Cal winked at her and picked up a piece. He turned it over in his hand a few times and then placed in the right spot with the first try.

"Hmm, so it seems, but you might have met your

match with me." She picked up another piece and placed it next to his piece.

"Yeah, she's pretty good, Uncle Cal," Tyler spoke up. "She put all of that together." He pointed to the right side of the puzzle.

"Well, I'm not surprised." Cal fixed his gaze on Carrie. "I knew she was amazing the moment I met her."

Soft pink flowed up Carrie's cheeks, and her eyes dropped to the puzzle. "I'm not that amazing."

Cal begged to differ, but he didn't want to make her uncomfortable. Silence fell as they raced to finish the puzzle first.

"Hah, I've got the last piece," Carrie teased as she held up the final jigsaw cutout.

He chuckled, enjoying the look of sheer happiness gracing her features. She finally looked relaxed and carefree, the way he remembered her six years ago. "You did a great job."

"No, *we* did a great job."

His heart flipped at the way she said 'we.' "You're right. We make a great team."

Her eyes locked with his and the surrounding sounds faded away for a moment. Just a moment. "We do, but we should head back. I need to check in with my assistant."

Just like that, the carefree look disappeared, replaced with a look of concern that Cal wanted to wipe away. "All right, I should check on Dexter and the herd again as well."

"Ah man, do you have to go?" Tyler asked.

"Yes, but I'll see you again in a few days." Cal ruffled his nephew's hair and gave him a side hug. "You too, Annie."

"Thank you for joining us," Stacy said as she entered the living room.

"Thank you for having me," Carrie said. "Maybe I'll see you again soon."

"We'd like that," Stacy said.

Cal gave her a hug and shook Jim's hand before extending his arm to Carrie. He wasn't sure she would take it, but after a slight hesitation, her skin touched his lighting a fire to his arm that traveled all the way up to his shoulder.

"Thank you for coming with me," Cal said as they reached the truck. He opened the door for her and helped her climb in.

"Of course. Your family is very nice, and it's not like you gave me much choice."

He smiled at her and shut her door before walking to the driver's side.

"I know they'd like to see more of you." He sneaked a glance as he started the truck.

"Mm." Carrie gave him a wistful smile before turning to look out the window.

Cal stifled a sigh as he pulled out of Stacy's drive and headed toward the inn. When they reached it, he turned off the ignition and stepped out to open Carrie's door. As her foot hit the pavement though, a voice carried out to them.

"Carrie? Where have you been?"

Carrie's head whipped toward the sound. "Philippe?" A tall man with dark hair and a hawkish nose stepped out of the shadows. "What are you doing here?"

"What am I doing here? You never called to let me know what was going on, so I felt the need to come check on you."

"I did call you when I arrived," Carrie said. "Your voicemail picked up, but I left a message. I figured you were busy since I didn't hear anything back."

The man's eyes flicked to Cal. "And I see you've been busy since then. Who is this?"

"I'm Cal," Cal said stepping forward. "I'm Carrie's husband." Cal wasn't certain why he said it other than he didn't like the guy, but he regretted the words the instant Carrie turned fiery, accusing eyes on him.

"Husband?" The man's brows inched up his forehead. "What's going on, Carrie?"

Carrie glared at Cal a moment longer before turning back to the man. "Technically, he's right, Philippe. When I was twenty-one, I went to Vegas with some friends. I must have had too much to drink because I married Cal. I came here to get the divorce papers signed. I'm sorry I didn't tell you."

"And it took you two days to get the papers signed?"

"Cal was being a little stubborn." Carrie's voice sounded stiff and forced, but Cal wasn't sure if it was because of what he'd said or because of the man.

"Probably after your money, no doubt." The man turned eyes as cold as ice Cal's direction.

Anger flared in his gut, but Cal took a deep breath to keep from punching the man. "I don't care a thing about Carrie's money."

The man's eyes shot fire at Cal before returning to Carrie. "Hey, what happens in Vegas stays in Vegas, right?"

Cal clenched his hands at his side. The man had completely ignored him - as if he weren't standing just a few feet away. And Cal hated that saying. Too many people used it to do things they wouldn't normally do and count them as okay.

"Yeah, you know how it is." Carrie shrugged her shoulders. "Young and stupid."

Carrie turned to Cal, but the expression in her eyes was unreadable. Still, he knew in that instant that anything they had built was gone. He would have to let her go and sign the papers.

"Carrie, I'll get the papers and bring them over in the

morning. Will that be soon enough?" The words pained him, and his stomach clenched.

"I'd rather we go tonight, Carrie. I have work tomorrow." The man grabbed her hand pulling her closer to him.

"No, we can go in the morning. I still need to pack and ready the plane." She turned back to Cal, but her eyes never met his. They appeared locked on the ground at his feet. "Thank you. If you could have those papers here at seven am tomorrow, I would greatly appreciate it."

"Of course." Cal tipped his hat first to Carrie and then to the man - the man he would remember forever as the one who stole Carrie from him. What made it even worse was the man's behavior. It seemed as though he tried to dominate and control Carrie, and it saddened Cal. She possessed such a fiery spirit, but it fizzled around this man. The smile and gaiety he had seen earlier had been erased with one word from the man's mouth. How could she marry him? Didn't she see how wrong they were for each other?

Cal left them there - two people who looked more like strangers than an engaged couple - and continued to his truck. As soon as he got inside, he turned his face upward. "Why God? Why would you bring her in my life only to take her away again? I've waited all these years, and I finally thought you were going to reconcile this relationship, and then this happens. I want to know why!"

Cal was surprised at the anger in his voice. He couldn't remember the last time he had raised his voice at anyone, much less at God.

"Trust me." The words filled his head, and Cal's anger softened. Trust. It was hard to do right now, but what other option did he have? He glanced back toward Carrie only to see them entering the inn together. Trust. It wouldn't be easy, but as that was all he could do, Cal took a deep breath and gave the situation over to God.

CHAPTER 13

*C*arrie woke early the next morning. Truth be told, she wasn't sure she had actually slept. After Cal left, she and Philippe had gone inside to secure him a room. Thankfully Dixie had been able to accommodate them. After that, they spent an hour down in the dining room. Philippe wanted details about the weekend, but Carrie managed to give him just enough information to satisfy him before turning the tables and asking him to tell her about his weekend. One thing Philippe loved was talking about his business. And as long as Cal came through with the papers, Carrie figured she might never have to tell Philippe all the details of the weekend.

After a shower, she finished packing her bag and scanned the room one last time to make sure she hadn't forgotten anything. A bittersweet feeling lay on her. She was glad to be going home, but a part of her knew she would miss this place. Miss Cal and his family even though ire still flowed through her when she thought of him informing Philippe of their marriage.

"Good morning, Carrie." Dixie looked up from the coffee carafe she was filling and greeted Carrie as she entered the dining room.

"Morning Dixie. Philippe and I will be checking out today if you want to get our receipts ready."

Dixie nodded, but her lips hinted at a sad smile. "I'm sorry to hear that. I hoped you might stick around a while, but I'll get right to it. Pancakes this morning again?"

"Sure." Carrie pushed back the sadness she felt at Dixie's words and filled a mug of coffee. Her table from yesterday was open, so she headed that direction. Only one other person sat in the dining room currently, and Carrie wondered how Dixie stayed in business.

"Well, it's quaint. I'll give it that."

Carrie looked up at Philippe as he set his mug down across from her. She smiled up at him as she asked, "How did you sleep?"

"Not as bad as I had expected, but I'm certainly ready for my own bed again. I don't know how you slept here two nights."

She took a sip of the satisfying warm beverage as she regarded him. "Oh, my bed was fine. I could have stayed longer."

Philippe stared at her, a concerned look on his face. "What happened to you out here?"

Carrie dropped her eyes to the mug. That was a good question, but she didn't have an answer for Philippe. It was probably just the lure of the small town, and she'd be back to her normal self as soon as she returned to New York.

"Here are your pancakes," Dixie said interrupting the uncomfortable silence.

"Thank you."

"Anything for you, sir?" Dixie turned her attention to Philippe.

"Just bacon and eggs for me if you have them."

"I'll be right back with them."

"Pancakes, Carrie? Since when do you eat pancakes?"

"I do on occasion." A movement outside the window caught her attention and she set her fork down. "Oh, I see Cal with the papers. I'll be right back." Before he could argue, she pushed her chair back and raced from the room.

She flung the front door open as he reached the top step. "Hey, Cal."

"Carrie." He tipped his hat, but his voice held none of its usual teasing inflection. "I've got the papers for you." He reached in his pocket and withdrew the familiar bundle of papers. "I hope you'll be very happy."

Carrie took the papers, not even glancing for a

signature. She could tell by the expression on his face he had signed them. "Cal," she began, but he shook his head.

"I don't understand why you are marrying him, but perhaps you're a different person in New York. I'm glad I got to see you again, even if only for a weekend."

Carrie's throat choked with tears. She hated that she was hurting him. "I'm glad I got to see you as well. Maybe-" She stopped. There was no use going down that road. She was going back to New York, and he was staying here. The chances they would ever meet again were slim to none. "Tell your family thank you again for everything."

Cal nodded and turned away, but Carrie caught the glistening of his eyes before he turned from her. She watched him get in his truck and fought her own tears, but it was better this way. At least that's what she needed to tell herself.

"Did you get it all taken care of?" Philippe asked as she returned to the table.

"Yep, all good," Carrie said with a tight smile. "I'll get these turned in and it should be finalized soon."

"Good, the sooner the better."

She dropped her eyes to the plate and blinked back the tears threatening to spill over. Crying in front of Philippe was not an option, and really, she was sure she'd be fine when she returned to New York. Life would pick back up like normal. She would design her wedding dress, plan her wedding, and get back to work. It would definitely keep her busy.

"Are you finished, Carrie? I'd like to get back to New York tonight."

"Sure." Carrie took the last bite of pancake and chewed slowly. She'd doubted many more pancakes would be in her future as she would need to get back to eating clean to fit in the dress she imagined wearing for her wedding.

They checked out with Dixie and then loaded their light luggage into the waiting car out front. Half an hour later, they were situated on the plane and heading home. Only then did Carrie realize she had forgotten to take Dixie's measurements.

*C*al pulled into his driveway and turned off the truck. He had firmly believed he would be able to remind Carrie of why they married, that she would change her mind about leaving, and they would have a life together, but instead she was gone. She was gone and the gaping hole in his heart was bigger than before.

"I wasn't expecting to see you today," Stacy said as Cal entered the hallway. Stacy often came over early to check the books and the orders. "Where's Carrie?"

"On her way back to New York with her fiancé."

Sympathy filled Stacy's eyes as she stood and walked to Cal. "I'm so sorry. I thought the way she looked at you last night that she was changing her mind."

Cal shrugged. He had thought many times over the weekend that he had changed her mind, but it hadn't turned out that way.

"What are you going to do now?" Stacy asked.

"The same thing I've always done. I'm going to work and pray and do my best to serve God."

"Cal-"

"Not now, Stacy. I've got chores to do. Might as well get to them." He continued past her to the backyard barely acknowledging Dexter when he jumped up on him. The world just didn't seem right anymore.

CHAPTER 14

ONE MONTH LATER

"*H*ow long are you going to mope around here?" Stacy put her hands on her hips and fixed him with her best 'snap out of it' expression.

"I'm not moping." Cal cinched the saddle under Ginger and smoothed out her skin to make sure it wasn't folded under the belt.

"What do you call it then? You barely eat. You've lost weight. Even Tyler and Annie have been asking why you never play with them anymore. It's been a month, Cal. When are you going to let her go?" She picked up the brush and ran it through Ginger's mane.

Cal took his hat off and ran his hand through his hair. "I don't know how to, Sis. Every bone in my body still tells me that we belong together."

"You haven't even tried to get over her. Why don't you

go out with Ginny and at least see if there's anything there? She's a nice girl, Cal. You could have a decent life with her."

A decent life. Cal didn't want a decent life. He wanted an amazing life, but he was certain that option had left when Carrie did. So, perhaps he should settle. Stacy was right. Ginny was nice and pretty, and she liked him. "Fine, the next time she comes by, I'll take her up on her offer."

"Good. I don't think you'll regret it." She finished the brushing and laid the brush back down.

Cal wasn't so sure about that, but he couldn't keep letting life pass him by. He'd wasted six years on Carrie. If he ever wanted to have a family - and he did - then he needed to move on. "We'll see." Cal walked Ginger out of the barn and then swung up on the saddle before heading out to move the cows. At least when he was riding, he still felt whole. This was where he belonged.

"That was a lovely dinner, Philippe," Carrie said as he opened the door of his BMW for her. It had been delicious, but Carrie couldn't keep her thoughts from straying back to the dinner Cal had cooked for her. Even though she had suggested they try cooking a meal together, Philippe had vetoed that idea insisting they had the money to go out or hire someone to cook for them.

"Yes, it was nice though our server was a little slow on her service. I would have left a much larger tip if she had refilled my glass quicker." He shut her door and walked to the driver's side.

"I'm sure she was doing her best," Carrie said softly. "The restaurant was busy."

"You're probably right." He started the car and backed out of the space. "Hey, let's move the wedding to June."

Carrie blinked at him. Was he joking? "June? That's only two months away, Philippe. That's not enough time to plan a decent wedding."

He glanced at her from the corner of his eye. "What are you talking about Carrie? With our money, we can make it happen as quickly as we want."

Our money. Carrie wondered just how much he was planning to contribute to the wedding. Her mother certainly had no money to give, so the majority would fall on Carrie's shoulders. "Okay, but what's the reason to speed it up?"

"I've been considering the idea since we got back, and I realized after seeing that other man that I don't want to chance losing you. I want to marry you as soon as possible, so we can start our life together."

"Well, I mean I can look around, but June is a busy wedding month, and I need enough time to make my dress."

"I don't care that much about the venue. Just find a place that can hold five hundred to a thousand people. I'm sure we'll get the same kind of publicity that Drew and Gwen did now that you're a billionaire as well. In fact, you should even get more because you're a female billionaire. Those don't happen every day."

Carrie winced at his sexist comment. Did he have any idea how chauvinistic he sounded? "They didn't ask for the publicity, Philippe. I think it's rather crass if we ask for it."

"Oh sure, sure, I just mean your wedding should be a headline story. Anyway, pick a good place and finish your dress. I can be ready pretty quickly. In fact, I'll have my tailor start on my tux tomorrow."

"Philippe, would you do a devotional with me tonight?" The words surprised even Carrie as they leapt out of her mouth. She had wanted to ask him since they returned from Soda Spurs, but every time she was about to ask, something kept her from it.

"A devotional? What do you mean?" His hands had tightened on the steering wheel and the stiffness in his posture matched the tone of his voice.

"I mean read the Bible and discuss it with me. I've been thinking it would be a good tradition to start."

"Where's this coming from, Carrie? You never wanted to do this before."

"To be honest, Cal did a devotional with me when I

was in Soda Spurs, and I really enjoyed it. I want it to be a part of my married life."

"Cal, huh?"

Carrie nodded. She hated mentioning Cal's name as it always made Philippe tense, but the devotional was one thing she had really enjoyed and wanted to continue.

"Sure, if it means that much to you, I'll try. I've never done one before though."

"We'll figure it out together," Carrie said.

CHAPTER 15

"Earth to Cal."

Cal shook his head to clear the woman from the past and focus on the woman in front of him. "Sorry, Ginny, what were you saying?" He set down his half-eaten sandwich to give her his full attention.

"I was saying we should try out the new movie theater in town. Sam said they are playing When Harry Met Sally, and that's one of my favorites." Ginny's lips formed a hopeful smile as she picked up her drink.

"Oh, yeah, sure, we could do that." This was his fourth date with Ginny, and while she was not Carrie, she was a nice woman. Still, no desire flamed within Cal for her the way it had with Carrie. He wondered if he would have to settle for a loveless marriage in order to start the family he longed for. He couldn't believe that was what God had planned for him, but he hadn't heard any wisdom from God on the Carrie front since the day she left.

Ginny sighed. "No, Cal, I don't think we can."

"What? What are you talking about, Ginny? I said we could. I can make time."

"It's not that, Cal; it's this." She motioned at the space between them. "We've tried dating for over a month, but I can tell your heart isn't in this. Half the time you're too busy to do something and when you aren't, your mind is a million miles away."

Cal raked a hand across his face. "I'm sorry, Ginny. You are an amazing woman, but you deserve more than I can give you. I'm afraid a woman stole my heart six years ago and I haven't been the same since."

"This is the woman you brought to church that one time, right? The pretty redhead?"

Cal nodded. "Yep, that's the one. Carrie."

"So, where is she now?"

A snort escaped Cal's mouth, and he reached into his pocket. His fingers touched on the envelope he had received in the mail yesterday. He withdrew it and tossed it on the table. "She's in New York about to marry the wrong guy."

Ginny picked up the envelope and peered inside. She withdrew the invitation first. "Carrie Bliss and Philippe Caron request the honor of your appearance June 15th at six pm?" She raised a brow at him. "She invited you to her wedding?"

Cal scoffed and shook his head. "No, there's more."

Ginny pulled a folded piece of paper out of the envelope and unfolded it. "Dear Cal, you don't know me, but I'm Gwen, Carrie's best friend. I'm not positive exactly what happened with you two in Soda Spurs, but she loves you. Please don't let her marry Philippe. It will be the worst mistake of her life. I've enclosed the invitation, so you know how much time you have. Gwen."

Ginny refolded the letter and tucked it and the invitation back in the envelope. "What are you still doing here, Cal?"

"What do you mean?"

"I mean the woman you love loves you and is about to marry another man. Her best friend is begging you to come and break up the wedding, and you're still here. Why?"

Cal shook his head. "Carrie left. She left me for him. I can't break that up. What if her friend is wrong?"

Ginny leaned back and crossed her arms. "I understand women are hard for men to figure out but let me let you in on a little secret. The best friend always knows best. This Carrie is probably fighting her feelings the same way you tried to and succeeding about as well I'd guess. I guarantee it will not be a wasted trip if you go out there."

Could he do that? Show up and break up a wedding? "I don't know, Ginny. Money is tight; I'm not sure I even have the money to get there. I'm about to have to sell half my herd to make my payments to the bank."

Ginny's eyes lit up. "Actually, you have the money to get there." She leaned down and pulled an envelope out of her purse and handed it to him.

"What is this?" he asked as he took the envelope. He folded back the lip and blinked at the check inside. It was made out to him for a thousand dollars.

A smile stole across Ginny's mouth. "I put up some of your wood carvings online. They sold like hotcakes. People love them, Cal."

Confusion clouded Cal's mind. People liked his carvings? Enough to buy them? "They sold, really?" His carvings were a hobby, not something he had ever considered doing for money.

"Of course they did." Ginny looked at him as if he'd lost his mind. "You are really talented, Cal. Anyway, that should be enough to cover a plane ticket. Then if you can get me some more carvings, I'll upload pictures of them. I bet if you could do a new piece a week then you could pay off your loan in no time."

Cal stared at the amazing woman across from him. A part of him wished he had developed feelings for her because she deserved someone amazing. "Why are you doing this for me, Ginny?"

Ginny shrugged. "While I wish there had been more between us, Cal, you are still my friend. Friends help friends. Now, go home, buy a ticket, pack, and go get your woman."

A surge of adrenaline flooded Cal. Maybe he could do this. He splayed his hands on the table top. "Okay, Ginny, I will."

*C*arrie zipped up the dress on the mannequin and stepped back to admire it. The dress hung perfectly with the trim barely gracing the floor, and the train pooled out in a perfect circle. It was beautiful to say the least.

"Carrie, it's breathtaking, but are you sure you want to get married so quickly?" Gwen folded her arms across her chest and sent Carrie a narrowed stare.

"Of course I want to get married." Carrie leaned closer and snipped a spare thread.

"Okay, let me rephrase that. I understand you want to get married, but so quickly? Have you forgotten about the misgivings you told me about?" Gwen stepped in front of the dress to capture Carrie's undivided attention.

Carrie bit her lip. Yes, there had been a few misgivings

with Philippe since they got back - the first being that he wanted to rush the wedding. Then there had been the devotional disaster. Though he had read them with her, there had been none of the connection she felt when she had done the same thing with Cal. Of course, it probably helped that Cal was much more knowledgeable in the word than Philippe was, so reading with him became a learning experience for her instead of just two people reading the Bible.

"I'm over those. Philippe is a great guy."

"He is." Gwen took Carrie's hand, "but he's not Cal. Are you sure you're over him?"

"What do you mean?" Carrie turned away to avoid Gwen's questioning eyes. "Lace, it needs just a little more lace."

"It doesn't need anything, Carrie," Gwen said coming up beside her. "I know you felt something for Cal when you were down there because you were different when you got back, and I saw that the way you looked at Philippe had changed. Are you sure you don't want to see him one more time before you go through with this marriage just to make sure?"

A giant sigh billowed out of Carrie's lips, and tears burned her eyes. "I already did, Gwen." She crossed to her desk and pulled a letter out of the drawer. It was thick and marked with the words 'Photos! Do Not Bend!'

"What is this?" Gwen asked as she took the envelope.

"It's from Dixie, the lady who ran the inn. I wrote to her saying I was interested if there were any properties for sale-"

"Wait, you're going back?"

Carrie shook her head annoyed at Gwen's interruption. "No, I was thinking about opening a boutique there and finding someone to run it. You should see their clothing selection. It's awful."

"You never told me you were thinking about that."

Was that hurt she heard in Gwen's voice? "I didn't tell anyone. I didn't want anyone to talk me out of it. Anyway, Dixie wrote me back that there's a shop for sale, but then she told me Cal was seeing someone else. She enclosed a few pictures."

Gwen returned her attention to the envelope and opened it. She scanned the letter first and then studied the two pictures. "Okay, so if this Dixie is correct, they haven't been dating long. I mean look at this picture. They aren't even touching." She turned the picture around and Carrie closed her eyes. She had studied the pictures enough when the letter first came in.

"He's with someone else." Carrie wiped a traitorous tear off her cheek. She was not going to cry. She had cried too much already. "I waited too long. He waited six years for me, but I guess when he finally signed the papers, he gave up on me."

"Oh, Carrie, I'm so sorry." Gwen's arms stole around

her, and that was all the tears needed to break the dam. One escaped and trickled down her cheek leaving a cold, wet trail.

"So, you see?" She sniffed against Gwen's shoulder. "Cal is out of the picture and it just makes sense to marry Philippe."

"Carrie, honey, it never makes sense to marry someone just because they are there. You should marry for love, and if you don't love Philippe-"

"I did marry for love once already." Carrie sucked back the rest of her tears and pulled away from Gwen. "I was stupid and wasted it, but I had my chance. Besides, I love Philippe." She stepped back toward the dress and looked at it with a critical eye. "Now, what do you think of this dress?"

Gwen sighed and stepped beside her. "I think it's amazing and you will look beautiful in it."

CHAPTER 16

*C*al looked at his watch and then out the window as if by looking out the window, he could encourage the plane to move faster or the hands of time to move slower. Why did there have to be a delay today? He was on a tight schedule as it was.

The elderly woman next to him touched his arm grabbing his attention. "You have a hot date?"

"Huh?"

"You've looked at your wristwatch seven times in the last ten minutes. I may be old, but I still have my eyes. Now, as far as I've seen in my life, only two things make a man as antsy as you are. Work and women, so which is it?"

Cal smiled. She must have a been a handful in her prime. "It's a woman. I have to go break up a wedding to win back the bride, and I know little about New York, but I fear I'm going to be too late."

The woman clucked softly. "Breaking up a wedding. Do you know she loves you back?"

"No, but my friend Ginny swears this shows she does." He reached into his pocket and pulled out the wedding invitation. It was crinkled from being in his pocket and starting to show its wear from the many times he had read and reread it.

The woman took the envelope and opened it. She scanned the invitation first and raised a thinned brow at him. Her expression changed, however, when she read the letter. "I find your friend Ginny very wise, but the Manhattan Penthouse is at least twenty minutes from the airport and that's if there's no traffic. Do you have a fallback plan in case we are late landing?"

Cal's face fell as he took back the invitation. "No, I hadn't expected to be delayed. I don't have Gwen's number and texting or calling Carrie just seems wrong."

"Well, I will pray everything works out for you then. And one more piece of advice."

Cal looked at her expectantly. She seemed knowledgeable about New York, so he would take whatever advice she doled out.

The woman looked to her left and then leaned closer. "Don't be nice getting off this plane. People in New York move quickly and walk over people if they have to. If you want to make it to the Manhattan Penthouse on time, you'll have to fight for it." She winked at him and patted his arm, and Cal chuckled.

"I'll do my best." The thought of pushing people out of his way to get off the plane first appalled him, but if it meant getting to Carrie on time, he would do it. He was sure his momma would understand and forgive him later.

Cal settled back into the seat, but he couldn't help one more glance at his wrist.

Carrie stared at her reflection in the mirror and tried to find her happiness. She might have convinced Gwen she was in love with Philippe yesterday, but she was having more trouble convincing herself today. Now that the wedding was actually here, the reality of what she was about to do sat on her shoulders like a weighted blanket.

"Another fantastic dress," Alyssa said over her shoulder.

Carrie's eyes flashed to the dark-haired woman behind her. She wore a deep purple empire waisted gown. Her dark hair was pulled up in an elaborate up do with only a few tendrils snaking down around her ears. A wide smile graced her delicate features. Motherhood suited her. Her face held a glow that Carrie only hoped hers would hold one day.

"That's because Carrie is an amazing designer," Gwen said joining Alyssa in the mirror's reflection. Gwen's gown was a match to Alyssa's, her red locks styled similarly. As with Gwen's wedding, Carrie had wanted them not only to look beautiful but to have a gown they might wear again.

Carrie turned to face her friends. "Thank you both. You are the most amazing friends any girl could have asked for."

"What about me?" Peyton spoke up from the couch. She had been playing with her favorite stuffed animal, but obviously didn't want to be forgotten.

"Of course, you are amazing," Carrie said with a laugh. Just like Gwen, she'd had no little sister or young female relative to ask to be her flower girl. Neither, it turned out, did Philippe. He was an only child as well.

"I can't wait until Michael is old enough to be a ring bearer. Then we can both walk down the aisle together." Peyton stood and twirled her dress.

The girls all chuckled, but the lighthearted topic did Carrie's heart good. "Honey, by the time Michael is mature enough to be a ring bearer, you'll probably be too old to be a flower girl," Alyssa said.

Peyton's eyes widened, and her mouth fell open. "There's an age limit on being a flower girl?"

"There is, but don't worry you have several years left."

Alyssa hugged the girl to her side. "I guess I better make more friends, so she can attend more weddings."

"Yes, you better," Gwen said. "I think she might find a way to make being a flower girl an occupation."

"I will." Peyton's head bobbed sending her tendrils shaking. Then her face scrunched up in confusion. "What's an occupation?"

Carrie joined in the laughter, but a little voice whispered in her head that she would never have this with Philippe. She realized she had never even had a discussion about children with him. Well, that wasn't true. She had brought it up once, but he had dismissed the conversation telling her that they would revisit it later. Surely, he would want children once they were married though.

"Well, I think it's about time," Gwen said checking her watch. "Are you ready?"

Carrie took a deep breath and checked the mirror one last time. Every hair was in place, her dress looked perfect, and the beautiful bouquet of purple tulips and stargazer lilies smelled heavenly. By all accounts, she was ready, but the nagging little doubt still tugged at her. Wedding jitters, she told herself, that's all it was. Wedding jitters.

"Yep, let's get me married." Carrie forced bravado in her voice and a smile on her face.

"You can still say no," Gwen whispered as they walked out the door.

"Everybody's here. It's too late."

"It's never too late. You simply say the words."

Carrie shook her head. She had lost Cal, and Philippe was a good man. They worked well together, and happiness would find them. She was sure of it. "They're waiting for us."

Gwen shook her head, a sad expression on her face, but she led the way down the hallway.

*f Cal had been a cursing man, he would have let loose a string of expletives as he checked his watch again. It was ten till six. He wouldn't make it before the wedding started. Probably not even by the time they asked if anyone had a reason these two should not be married. All he could hope for was that he would get there before they said 'I do.'

"Welcome to La Guardia airport, ladies and gentlemen. It's been our pleasure to serve you on this flight. The local time is five fifty pm. We'll be taxiing to the gate for the next few minutes, so please stay in your seats with your seatbelts fastened until you see the illumination go off. Bags will be at carousel seven and there will be people to assist you if you need help with a connecting flight. We know you have a choice when you fly, and we thank you for flying United Airlines."

The pilot's announcement did nothing but ramp up

the anxiousness in Cal's heart. Another few minutes to taxi? He was going to be so late. At least he didn't have to stop at baggage claim. With the knowledge that his trip would be short, he had only packed an emergency bag with a change of clothes, toothbrush and toothpaste, and deodorant. That way if he did get stuck somewhere, he'd at least be covered for a day.

The elderly woman, who had introduced herself as Ethel earlier, touched his arm. "Remember, this is not the time to be nice. Go get your girl."

One side of his lip pulled into a crooked grin. "I'll try, Ethel." Cal's eyes stayed glued to the overhead display. As soon as the light went off and the ding sounded, Cal grabbed his bag and stood, hunching down from the low ceiling. Ethel scooted over to his side, so he would be even closer to the aisle. The man sitting in the aisle seat glared up at him as he pushed his glasses up his nose. A businessman by the look of his fitted suit.

"Sorry," Cal said to the man, "love waits for no man." Cal was close enough to see the stewardess when she opened the door, and he pushed past the spectacled man into the aisle.

"Thank you for flying with us," the stewardess said, but Cal was already past her and heading up the ramp. By the time it opened into the expansive airport, he was practically jogging. His eyes scanned the large screens in search of ground transportation. When he finally saw the sign he wanted, he hurried that direction. Cal chanced a glance at his watch and shook his head. The only chance he had of stopping this wedding was with a miracle.

🌸

Outside the grand doors, Carrie's mother, who was standing in for her father, and Philippe's two friends stood waiting for them. Carrie noticed how much grayer her mother's hair was than the last time she had seen her.

"Wow, Carrie," her mother said taking her free hand, "you did a wonderful job on this dress. It's amazing."

Carrie looked down at her mother's weathered hand. She hadn't had to take up hard labor after Carrie's father passed, but it was clear she had been doing some work as her hands had aged much more than Carrie remembered. Maybe she should send more money to her mother to help her out. "Thanks Mom, I just wish Dad were here to see it."

"Your Dad is watching from Heaven, Carrie, and he's so proud of you. As am I." Her mother pulled Carrie in for a hug and Carrie smiled at the scent of Vanilla and sugar. At least she hadn't given up her love of baking.

The music began then and David, one of the Groomsmen, looked to the rest of the group. "Everybody ready?"

Gwen flashed Carrie one more 'are you sure' look, but Carrie ignored it and nodded to David. "Let's do this."

David opened the door to the grand ballroom and held out his hand for Alyssa. With a smile, she tucked her arm through his and they stepped into the large room. Peter, the best man, and Gwen went next. Then Peyton followed.

"Are you sure you want to do this?" Her mother fixed her with an intense stare as she squeezed her hand.

"Why does everyone keep asking me that?" Carrie asked. Her heart pounded in her chest and her breath felt short. Nerves, it was just nerves. If everyone would quit asking her if she was sure, then Carrie was sure her heart would return to its normal rhythm and her breath would come normally.

"I saw the look you shared with Gwen. I may not be around you much anymore, but she is. This is marriage, Carrie. You should be sure."

Carrie swallowed her irritation. This was supposed to be the happiest day of her life, and it would be if everyone would support her and stop questioning her. "I'm sure, Mom." The wedding march began to play, and Carrie pulled back her shoulders. "Now, that's our cue, so let's get to it."

Her mother's lips pulled into a tight line as if she didn't believe Carrie, but she followed her lead as they stepped onto the red carpeted train that led into the grand ballroom. The ballroom looked amazing lighted up with the white Christmas lights, the large windows held fantastic views of the city lights, and Philippe looked as handsome as ever standing up front with the wedding party.

Hundreds of guests filled both sides of the aisle and camera bulbs flashed with each step she took. Carrie hadn't expected this many photographers, but this had to be Philippe's doing. He had wanted the wedding to be everywhere. Carrie's cheeks hurt from her plastered smile, but there was no way she would be caught on camera with anything less than a smile.

Her feet carried her forward even though the voice in her head urged louder for her to turn around, to bolt for the door. Before she knew it, she had handed off the bouquet and was taking Philippe's hands in front of the minister.

*C*al stepped out of the airport and on to the busy ground transportation area. Though still warm, the air had cooled when the sun set and evening hit. Cal's eyes widened at the number of cars lined up and darting in and out of traffic, but he had no time to linger on the immensity of it.

He hurried to a waiting cab and slid into the back seat. "Can you take me to the Manhattan Penthouse?"

"Of course." The cab driver punched a button and then pulled into the stream of traffic. Cal scrambled to buckle his seat belt as the car weaved in and out. How in the world did Carrie live here? The traffic alone would drive him crazy. His insides were coiled tighter than Dick's hatband.

As the cab left the airport, Cal was assaulted with the visual imagery of all the lights. Now, this he understood someone being intoxicated by. The lights competed for his attention at every turn. Focus, he said to himself sparing another glance at his watch. "Please, can you hurry," Cal urged the cab driver. The wedding had already started, and with every ticking second, he felt Carrie slipping further from his grasp.

*P*hilippe's smile appeared off, forced. Or was it Carrie's imagination? Had the misgivings of her friend and mother started to rub off on her?

"Dear friends," the minister began, "we are gathered here today in the sight of God, and the presence of friends and loved ones, to celebrate one of life's greatest moments. We are here to give recognition to the beauty of love that is shared between Philippe and Carrie as they complete their family in holy matrimony."

No, it was not her imagination. His face had tightened at the word love. Was he having second thoughts as well?

The minister continued his speech. "Marriage is a contract that is not to be entered into lightly but thoughtfully and seriously. There needs to be a deep realization of the obligations and responsibilities it carries. Marriage is the moment where two hearts and souls are joined together for eternity."

This time Carrie's face twitched. A contract. Binding. Obligations. Responsibilities. The words assaulted her and sent her mind swirling back to this moment six years ago. She remembered no hesitation then even though she'd been in an all-night wedding chapel with a man she barely knew. So, why was there such hesitation now?

As if far away, Carrie heard the minister pray, but her mind refused to focus on the words. The presence of slick sweat grabbed her attention, and she glanced down at her hand joined with Philippe's. Was that his sweat or hers?

"The joining of two hearts as husband and wife is a commitment like no other. It offers opportunities for sharing and for personal growth that no other human relationship can equal. A husband and wife are each other's best friends, confidants, lovers, teachers, listeners and critics."

Teachers? Was that why she felt much more of a bond

with Cal when they read the devotional? Because in that area, he was her teacher? In fact, in all things religious, she presumed Cal would be a teacher. Carrie forced her mind away from Cal. Surely, Philippe could be a teacher too, but Carrie had no idea what he could teach her. Her eyes rose from their clasped hands to his face, but his eyes weren't focused on her. They were focused on something to his left. Carrie turned to follow his gaze.

He was staring at the clock. Was he so bored that he couldn't wait to leave his own wedding? Could she marry a man who was so impatient? She thought of Cal and his cool ease. He never seemed impatient for anything.

"The bond between a husband and wife deepens and enriches every fact of life. Happiness is fuller, and commitments are stronger. Marriage also encourages new life and new experiences and finds new ways of expressing love through the ups and downs of life. Philippe and Carrie as your journey begins as husband and wife, I would ask you both remember to always treat each other with respect and remind yourself often of what brought you here today."

"I object."

A collective gasp erupted in the room, and all eyes turned to the voice who had broken the solemnity of the ceremony.

CHAPTER 17

"Young lady, I didn't ask for objections." The minister's stern voice surprised Carrie as he regarded the perpetrator.

"I am aware of that," Gwen said stepping forward, "but I can't let this continue." She glanced briefly at the gathered guests, her face as red as her hair. "Carrie, I know you think it's not a big deal and that you don't deserve love or something, but I can't let you marry Philippe." She turned to Philippe. "Sorry, she does care for you, but she loves someone even more."

Philippe's eyes widened, and his mouth fell open, but no words escaped.

"Carrie, you belong with Cal. Perhaps you weren't supposed to be together six years ago when you first married, but I saw you when you came back. You were different, happier. You belong with him."

Carrie blinked. How was this possible? Her best friend was ruining her ceremony. "Gwen, I told you he's with someone else."

"He's only with her because he thinks he lost you," Gwen pushed.

"You can't know that," Carrie said. "You haven't even met him."

"He sent you a letter every year on your anniversary. That's not the actions of a man who would jump into another relationship. Those pictures prove nothing-"

"Wait, what pictures?" Philippe had found his voice and it was filled with confusion and maybe a hint of anger.

"I-" Carrie glared at Gwen before turning to Philippe. What should she say? Opening a branch there had made sense at the time, but Carrie realized how awful it would look now. She decided on the truth. Gwen was right. Lies of omission were just as bad as outright lies. They had created quite a mess. "A few days ago, I wrote to Dixie, the inn owner, about opening a shop there. I wasn't planning to run it, just find someone who would. In the letter, I also asked her about Cal. I suppose I was having reservations, Philippe." She shook her head unable to believe these words were coming out of her mouth. "I was certain I didn't care for Cal, but when I saw pictures of him with someone else, feelings surfaced or resurfaced, I guess. My brain wanted to convince my heart I hadn't cared for him all these years, but the truth was that I loved him and that's why I ran from commitment before."

Philippe opened his mouth to speak, but he was interrupted by a voice from the guests. "I object too."

Carrie turned to see Sierra standing and making her way to the stage. "I can't let this marriage happen either."

"Why not?" Carrie had no idea if the words issued from her mouth, Gwen's, or Phillips's as they all seemed to speak at the same time.

"Carrie, you can't marry him. He's only marrying you for your money."

"What?" This time the word clearly came from Philippe, and he was indignant.

Sierra glanced nervously at Philippe before continuing. "Don't get me wrong, he might really care for you, but I overheard him outside the shop one day talking about how he was pushing up the wedding date to gain access to your money. Evidently his company isn't doing so good."

Carrie turned to face Philippe. "Is that true?"

His face paled and his Adam's Apple bobbed several times as he swallowed. His eyes shifted to the left and right before finally landing on Carrie's. "It's true that my company is having some financial issues, and I do care for you, but I proposed after I got wind of your net worth increasing."

"You proposed the very night I found out, how could you have known?" Carrie's mind reeled with this knowledge. Philippe didn't love her. She had divorced a man who loved her and almost married a man who didn't. What was wrong with her?

"I had someone keeping tabs on your business. You had more orders coming in and your stock was rising, so I figured it was a good time to propose. I wasn't positive until I found the letter you stashed under the register."

Carrie's mouth dropped open. "You snooped in my shop?"

He shrugged. "I wasn't snooping. I was confirming suspicions. You shoved something under the register that night when I entered your shop. Figured I'd take a look at what you didn't want to show me. I hoped as a billionaire you wouldn't mind helping your husband's company out, but to tell you the truth, I'm glad your assistant said something. I really don't want to be shackled in a marriage."

Shackled? Who was this man in front of her? She opened her mouth to retort, but before she could, another voice spoke up.

"I object to this marriage."

"Oh, good grief," the minister said throwing up his hands. "What now?"

*C*al blinked up at the expansive white building looming in front of him. He hoped it had an elevator because even in his good condition, it would take him way too long to get to the top if he had to take the stairs.

He opened the door and scanned for the elevator sign. Thankfully, he found it near the back of the room. With wide and purposeful steps, he strode that direction, his boots echoing on the marble flooring. He pressed the button, surprised to find his finger shaking.

As the door opened and he stepped inside, he practiced the words he would say in his head. Nothing sounded right, and by the time the doors opened, he had decided simple would be best.

A small sign announced the Bliss Caron wedding outside a room with large oak doors. Praying he wasn't too late, Cal pulled the doors open. "I object to this wedding."

As the silence fell, Cal took in the enormous room for the first time. There had to be hundreds of people in the room and every eye focused on him.

"Cal?" Carrie's voice carried from the stage and Cal focused on it. She wasn't holding hands with the groom, so perhaps he wasn't too late. Camera bulbs flashed as he made his way up the red carpeted aisle, but he ignored them. He was nobody, so he imagined they wouldn't care about him nor did he care if they ran an article about him.

"Carrie, I hope I'm not too late, but you can't marry him. I may have signed the divorce papers, but I never should have. Without you, I'm lost. Even more so now that I got to have you back in my life for a few days. I'll do whatever it takes to show you that we belong together."

Carrie's lips twitched and then broke out into a full grin. "I feared I had lost you, Cal."

"Lost me? What are you talking about?"

"I wrote Dixie asking about you. She sent me pictures of you with some blond."

Cal's lips twitched into a sideways smile. "That was Ginny. She's a sweet girl and Stacy convinced me to give her a chance after you left, but there was nothing there. My heart belongs to you. It has since that night in Vegas."

Carrie's eyes filled with moisture. "My heart belongs with you too. I was stubborn and didn't want to believe it, but I see it now."

"Great, is someone going to get married today?" the minister asked.

"We don't have a marriage license," Carrie began.

"But we could have a ceremony and make it official later," Cal continued.

"I was thinking the same thing." Carrie flashed a conspiratorial wink at him.

"Fine, can we do the ceremony then? I do have another engagement to attend."

"Philippe, would you mind taking a seat?" The words came from the redheaded woman next to Carrie, and Cal figured it had to be Gwen. He had never met the woman, but he liked her spunk.

"Gwen!" Carrie was clearly shocked at her friend's behavior.

Gwen simply shrugged. "You aren't marrying him. Cal needs a place to stand."

Cal ducked his head as a laugh bubbled up inside of him. Though Carrie had spoken of Gwen, she had failed to mention the spunk of her friend. Philippe turned a shade of red, but he took a seat in the congregation along with his two groomsmen.

"Drew and Max, why don't you come stand up here for Cal?"

Cal turned to see who Gwen was talking to. Two men from the front row stood up. One held a baby in a pack on his chest. Both were dressed nicely in designer suits.

"Hey, Cal, nice to meet you. I'm Drew Devonshire. I belong to the feisty one." He flashed a wink at Gwen before shaking Cal's hand.

"You have your hands full," Cal said softly.

Drew chuckled. "You're telling me."

The man with the baby stepped forward next. "I'm

Maxwell Banks. I'm married to Alyssa there." He pointed at the beautiful brunette standing beside Gwen.

Cal shook his hand. "Thank you both for standing in."

"Our pleasure. These three are thick as thieves now. If you're marrying into this den, then we'll see a lot more of each other."

A brief moment of hesitation flashed through Cal. These men were a different class than he was. He couldn't imagine much commonality existed between them, but Carrie was his focus. If these men came with her, then so be it. He would acclimate to whatever he had to.

The men shuffled into place and Gwen stepped back behind Carrie. Cal took the newly vacated spot next to Carrie and grasped her hands. The minister raised his eyebrow as if asking if they were ready. Cal and Carrie nodded and then shared a smile.

"Okay, so even though this won't be a legally binding ceremony, we are gathered here today to witness a wedding between Carrie Bliss and-" he paused before leaning toward Cal - "I didn't catch your name."

"Cal Roper."

The minister nodded and leaned back again. "Between Carrie Bliss and Cal Roper. I don't know these two well, but it appears they have a history and are not entering this union lightly. May God bless this union and may no one else object."

A titter of laughter spread through the guests. Though

probably not the wedding Carrie had dreamed of, Cal could think of nothing better. It was real and imperfect, just like the two of them.

"Carrie, do you take Cal to be your lawfully wedded husband to have and to hold, to honor and cherish, forsaking all others until death do you part?"

"I do." Carrie accented her words with a light squeeze on his hands.

"Cal, do you take Carrie to be your lawfully wedded wife to have and to hold, to honor and cherish, forsaking all others until death do you part?"

"I do."

"Do you have the rings?"

Carrie's eyes widened. "Oh no, the rings."

Cal grinned as he held up a finger. He reached into his shirt pocket and pulled out the simple silver bands they had gotten married with in Vegas six years ago. "I know it's not much, and I promise I'll get you a better ring soon, but these hold a lot of promise." He handed his ring to her.

"You kept them all this time?" Her eyes sparkled with the wet sheen filling them.

"I told you I knew then, and I hoped one day you would wear it again."

"Take notes kid," he heard Max say softly behind him, "that's how you win a girl's heart."

"Carrie, please place the ring on Cal's hand and say, with this ring I thee wed."

Carrie slid the band on Cal's finger. "With this ring I thee wed." Her voice was choked with emotion and so soft that Cal doubted many in the audience heard it.

"Cal, will you do the same?"

Cal slipped the silver ring on Carrie's finger and repeated the phrase.

"Well, without a marriage certificate, I have no authority here, but I believe that soon this union will be legal, so I pronounce you man and wife to be."

Another chuckle circulated through the crowd and Cal felt laughter bubble up inside him as well.

"You may kiss the bride."

Cal wasted no time in pulling Carrie to him, circling her waist and claiming her lips.

CHAPTER 18

"I was thinking it would be amazing if we flew back to Vegas to get married legally," Carrie said as they danced across the hardwood floor.

After the ceremony, they had walked across the hall to the reception area. The room was set up with a full bar and tables with elegant white cloths and fine china. They enjoyed a dinner of prime rib and vegetables before stepping onto the dance floor for their first dance.

Cal bit his lip as he turned Carrie around. He had been hoping to avoid this conversation as long as possible, but as she brought it up, he figured it was time to come clean. "Carrie, there's something I need to tell you. It was a rough year last year. It forced me to take an extra loan out from the bank. I don't have the money to repay it much less take a trip to Vegas." He looked down at her surprised to see her smiling. "What? Why are you smiling?"

Carrie chuckled. "Cal, look around." He scanned the room wondering what he was looking for. "I paid for this, Cal. The room, the food, the flowers."

"You mean your mother paid for it." Cal's brow wrinkled in confusion.

"No, Cal, I mean I paid for it. I'm a billionaire. So is Max and so is Drew."

Billionaire? The word did not compute in his rancher brain. How much money formed a billion anyway? "A billionaire? I knew you had money, but I had no idea."

Carrie nodded. "Yep, I have more than enough money to pay off your loan and fly us to Vegas."

The chivalrous need to take care of his wife flared within Cal. "But, I can't let you pay off my loan. That was my own fault."

"Technically, we were married when you accrued that debt, so what's yours is mine. Besides, you're not letting me do anything." Carrie placed a hand on his cheek. "My money is your money. You know two become one and everything."

Cal still didn't feel right taking her money, but he also knew he wouldn't win this argument. She had a stubborn streak, and he was man enough not to let money ruin their relationship. "I still plan on working," he said with a smile.

"I wouldn't have it any other way. You are quite sexy

on the back of the horse, and I'd like to keep seeing that image."

His face clouded. "That reminds me, Carrie. We do need to talk about living arrangements." They'd been so caught up in the wedding that they had forgotten some of the real details that could pose a problem. Like the fact that she lived hundreds of miles away, and he didn't want to give up his ranch.

She smiled and shook her head. "No, we don't. I told you I wrote Dixie to ask about you, but that was only part of why I wrote her. I asked her to search around for a shop I could purchase so I could open a branch in Soda Spurs."

Cal blinked at her as he let the information sink in. "You planned to come back?"

"No, I planned to hire someone to run it, but I think the women of Soda Spurs need someone who knows the beauty of the town."

Cal didn't know what to say. His heart felt like it was going to burst. He had only dreamed of this day for six years, and the reality was so much better. He pulled Carrie closer to him. "I love you, Carrie Bliss."

"I love you too, but I believe the name is Carrie Roper now though I may have to keep Carrie Bliss on my designs."

Cal chuckled as he lowered his lips to Carrie's. Always the business head with her, but he didn't care what name was on her designs as long as he got to call her his wife.

"*I*s everybody in?" Carrie asked as she looked around the limo. After the wedding, she had decided she didn't want to wait to marry Cal again and had asked the wedding party to join her on a quick trip to Vegas. What better way to remarry the man of her dreams than recreating their first marriage?

After a quick stop in Soda Spurs to pick up Stacy and her family, they had re-boarded the jet and landed in Vegas a few hours later. Their first stop had been to get the marriage license which thankfully went off without a hitch. Now, they were on their way to the strip. Though Carrie wasn't sure the original minister who married them was still practicing, she was certain the chapel would still be open.

"Where to?" the driver asked.

"Chapel of the Heart," Cal and Carrie said together and shared a smile.

"I've never seen so many lights," Annie said her face pressed to the window.

"Yeah, this is pretty cool." Peyton's face was also pressed to the window right next to Annie's. The two had become fast friends on the plane ride over and Carrie was fairly certain a reunion existed in their future.

"There it is," Trevor shouted as a large neon red heart with a white cross through it came into view.

Carrie squeezed Cal's hand as the limo pulled to a stop. "You ready to do this?"

"I've never been readier for anything in my life."

The doors opened, and the group piled out. Carrie laughed at the sheer size of their party. She doubted the chapel was used to having this many people there.

"Can I help-" the woman's voice stalled as she looked up from the book she had been writing in. "My, there's an awful lot of you."

"But just two of us to get married," Cal said stepping forward. "Can you tell me if Dave Nichols is still a minister here?"

"You remember his name?" Carrie asked quietly.

Cal smiled at her. "I remember everything."

"Yes, Dave Nichols is still here and working tonight as it turns out," the woman said.

"Great. We'd like him to marry us as soon as possible."

The woman smiled and consulted her book. "Well, how about right now? Give me five minutes and I'll ready the chapel."

She disappeared into the room and a few minutes later the door swung open. The chapel was almost exactly as Carrie remembered though the carpets looked newer like they had been replaced recently. She took her place next to Cal at the front and clasped his hands.

"I may be getting older, but I tend to remember the names of the couples I have married, and I seem to remember that I already married you two once. Is that right?"

Cal laughed, and Carrie dropped her eyes to the floor as a heat crawled up her neck. She hadn't expected the minister to remember them. "You are correct, Sir. We were serious the first time, but life kind of got in the way. However, we have straightened out the life part, and we'd like you to marry us again."

The minister smiled. His face looked exactly the same under his Elvis wig though his jumpsuit seemed to fit a little tighter. "Well, I am not one to stand in the Big Guy's way. How about we get this remedied?"

The wedding party circled around Cal and Carrie as the minister began the ceremony. What a stark contrast from The Manhattan Penthouse she had been at just hours before, but Carrie wouldn't change it for the world. Somehow, this seemed right - the perfect place for her marriage with Cal to begin. Again.

"By the power vested to me by Elvis, God, and the great state of Nevada, I now pronounce you husband and wife. You may kiss your bride. Thank you very much."

Carrie smiled as she leaned forward and met Cal's lips. She wasn't sure exactly what the future would hold, but she was ready for whatever lay ahead in the next chapter as long as it included Cal.

The End!

IT'S NOT QUITE THE END!

Thank you so much for reading *The Billionaire's Cowboy Groom*. So Carrie and Cal had their wedding, and we got to see all the other billionaires again. I thought this would be the end of the billionaire series, but as I was working on my new series, The Blushing Brides, my cover designer messed up and used the template from the Billionaires series. I was in a time crunch, so instead of having her redo everything, I decided there was at least one more billionaire story in me, and I just had her change the title. I think this one will be fun, and I'm planning a little sass!

I hope you enjoyed the story as well. If you did, would you

do me a favor? If you did, please leave a review. It really helps. It doesn't have to be long - just a few words to help other readers know what they're getting.

I'd love to hear from you, not only about this story, but about the characters or stories you'd like read in the future. I'm always looking for new ideas and if I use one of your characters or stories, I'll send you a free ebook and paperback of the book with a special dedication. Write to me at loranahoopes@gmail.com. And if you'd like to see what's coming next, be sure to stop by authorloranahoopes.com

I also have a weekly newsletter that contains many wonderful things like pictures of my adorable children, chances to win awesome prizes, new releases and sales I might be holding, great books from other authors, and anything else that strikes my fancy and that I think you would enjoy. I'll even send you the first chapter of my newest (maybe not even released yet) book if you'd like to sign up.

Even better, I solemnly swear to only send out one newsletter a week (usually on Tuesday unless life gets in the way which with three kids it usually does). I will not spam you, sell your email address to solicitors or anyone else, or any of those other terrible things.

This series will be continued, but for now, would you like to meet some characters for a new series.

NOT READY TO SAY GOODBYE YET?

*H*ave we seen the last of Carrie and Cal? I doubt it, but be sure to preorder your copy of The Cowboy Billionaire to meet Hunter Garrison and Daisy Keller. Two opposites forced to team up to help each other. Sparks will fly, but will love bloom?

And while you're waiting on that story, why not take a chance on The Cowboy's Reality Bride.

The Cowboy's Reality Bride

He just wants to marry and settle down...

But all the women he's dated want more than a small town and a simple ranch life which is why he allows himself to be talked into auditioning for a reality dating show. He never thought he'd actually get picked.

She is trying to run from her past...

When Laney gets fired from her job, she is free to help her friend out, but she thought she was just doing makeup.

Who wants to play by the rules....

Laney is instantly attracted to Tyler, and he might feel

the same, but there's just one problem. She's not a contestant!

Read on for a taste of The Cowboy's Reality Bride....

THE COWBOY'S REALITY BRIDE PREVIEW

*L*aney Swann clutched her designer bag tighter as she weaved in and out of the crowded sidewalk. Why did the crowd have to be so thick today, on the one day she overslept? Normally, she was out the door by six am giving her plenty of time to get uptown, stop at the coffee shop, and make it to work by eight, but sleep had eluded her last night, and she'd slept through her alarm. Now, she was paying the price.

She flipped her delicate silver watch around to read the face and quickened her pace. Time was not on her side today. She was going to be so late, and Victoria Bonavich detested tardiness. It was a fireable offense in her book if you stepped in the office even a minute late, and Laney couldn't afford to lose this job. She'd moved to the city with big dreams but a small savings after college.

Without this job, there would be no paying her rent, and she'd have to go home. A nervous spring coiled in her stomach. She couldn't lose this job.

"Watch it," a man's voice cried out as she squeezed between him and another man with a cell phone glued to his ear.

"Sorry," she called back, but her head never turned. Turning around would cost her precious seconds and she had none to spare. Her heart was thudding a constant drum of the precious seconds slipping away.

A tendril of blond hair appeared in her vision and she blew it off her forehead. Great. Now, not only was she late, but her hair was eking out of its sprayed mold, another issue she would have to remedy before seeing Madame Bonavich or The Man-eater as they called her in the office.

The woman was fearsome. With short grey hair, hawkish eyes, and thin lips which rarely smiled, she exuded a no-nonsense air wherever she went, but Laney enjoyed working for her. Mostly. She had learned so much in the six months she had been at this agency even though she was still just an unknown assistant to Madame Bonavich. Actually, she had learned so much more from Myra, the makeup artist she assisted before photo shoots, but Laney still hoped to become Madame Bonavich's assistant one day. Then she would have a chance at becoming a well-known makeup artist herself. At least she had received the promotion to coffee gopher the last month. It gave her a chance to interact with The Man-eater if only for a minute.

However, today, it could be her downfall. Only fifteen minutes remained to obtain the coffee and return to the office, and it wasn't looking good. Laney stepped up her pace a little more. Not too fast though. The last thing she wanted to do was trip, and sadly, she was a bit of a klutz.

"Excuse me," she said as she pushed through another clump of pedestrians. Why did it seem as if people walked slower and in impenetrable groups whenever she was in a hurry? The busy city was always like this, she knew that, but her need to move at a faster pace exaggerated the normal bustling bog and edged her anxiety up another notch.

At last the coffee shop came into view. Sweet relief flowed over her even though her feet ached already from the rigorous pace she had set the moment she stepped out of her door. The four-inch heels were a requirement in the agency - something that had taken Laney months to get used to - and though she agreed they added style to her outfit, her feet were not fans. They screamed for a nightly soak, and she had purchased so much Epsom Salt in the last few months she should buy stock in the company.

A sigh billowed out of her lips as she pulled open the door, and the spring coiled tighter. At least four other people stood in line. Laney bit her lip and checked her watch again. Thirteen minutes remained. Her foot began a rhythmic cadence on the floor, the impatient tapping garnering a few irritated stares, but Laney didn't care. She didn't have time to care.

The man in front of her turned around. "You appear to be in an awful hurry. Would you like to take my spot?"

"Could I? That would be amazing." Laney stepped in front of the man but remained facing him. He had the most arresting eyes. "My boss is a bit of a time manager, if you know what I mean. If I don't get her coffee and get back to her in just over ten minutes," she blew out a puff of air, "I don't even know what will happen, but it won't be good."

The man said nothing, just raised an eyebrow at her, but Laney couldn't shut her mouth. Perhaps it was his beautiful blue eyes - she had always been a sucker for blue eyes.

"Normally, it's not an issue, but last night sleep evaded me. I just tossed and turned, so when my alarm clock rang, I guess I didn't hear it. Though I must have turned it off because it wasn't still going off when I did finally wake up. Sadly, by then, I was running late, and now I'm in danger of incurring her wrath." Laney paused as the man's lips pulled into a smirk. "What?"

He pointed behind her toward the register. "I believe it's your turn to order."

"Oh, right, thank you." A heated flush crawled up her

face as she turned to face the woman behind the counter. She had made a fool of herself with the handsome man behind her. Why did her mouth always seem to run unchecked whenever she was nervous?

"Can I help you?"

"Yes, I uh..." Laney cleared her throat and forced her mind to focus. She could berate herself later. "I need a tall caramel macchiato and-" she shook her head. Even after a month, she didn't have Madame Bonavich's order memorized, but who could blame her? It had to be the longest order she had ever seen. "Sorry, just a second." Her fingers rifled in her purse until they touched a folded piece of paper. She pulled it out and unfolded it. "A double ristretto venti half soy nonfat organic chocolate brownie iced vanilla double shot gingerbread Frappuccino extra hot with foam upside down double blended, one Sweet N Low and one NutraSweet."

The cashier blinked, and a momentary shell-shocked expression covered her face. Then composure set in and she rang up the order and picked up two cups. Laney felt sorry for the woman. She merely had to read off an order, but this woman had to put that nonsense on a cup in a way that the barista making the coffee would understand. Not for the first time, Laney wondered if Madame Bonavich ordered this drink because she enjoyed it or because she relished putting others through the ringer.

With the bill paid, Laney continued down the line to

stand at the other end where the barista placed completed drinks. She kept her eyes on the floor to avoid seeking the nice man again. He didn't need another verbal diatribe from her.

Nine more minutes. She was cutting it so close. The office was just around the corner, but her high heels kept her from running, so she'd have to opt for long strides and hope for the best.

"Caramel Macchiato and gingerbread frap," the barista called as she placed the two drinks down.

"Thank you." Laney flashed the woman an apologetic smile as she grabbed the drinks.

As she pushed open the door, she realized she should have asked for a tray. A cup in each hand made it nearly impossible to adjust her purse strap which kept threatening to slip off her shoulder with every step. Unable to stop, Laney adjusted her body by throwing her right shoulder as high into the air as possible in hopes gravity would keep the purse strap there.

She must look a sight, hunched over to one side. Madame Bonavich would blow her lid if she saw Laney, but it was this or arrive late with the woman's coffee, and Laney honestly didn't know which would be worse.

A sigh of relief spilled from her mouth as the office came into view. She would not chance looking at her watch, but she figured she had a few minutes to spare. However, she also had a conundrum. How was she going to open the door? She hated taking the chance but stacking one cup on top of the other appeared to be the quickest option.

Before her mind changed, she set the venti on top of her cup and secured it with her chin. Then she reached for the door handle, but as her fingertips brushed the cold metal, the door swung open.

The force knocked her backwards. Her chin lifted from the lid of the cup, and without something to secure it, it teetered. Laney observed in slow-motion horror as the cup not only fell off its perch but onto her chest. The lid popped off and flew through the air as the contents of the drink spilled down Laney's front.

Her body finally unfroze when the searing hot liquid broached her skin. Laney jumped farther back sending the venti cup crashing to the pavement.

"I'm so sorry. Can I help?"

Anger flared in her stomach, and Laney flicked her eyes up to take in the perpetrator before she let loose her vitriol on him. However, the flame fizzled at the sight of the young man with glasses who stood gaping at her. His wide eyes held an apology and his baby face placed his age in his early twenties - probably a college intern. She swallowed the harsh words she wanted to bark at him. If she'd had Madame Bonavich's coffee order written anywhere else, she would give him the paper and tell him to go replace the coffee. It would be late, but perhaps late was better than never, but she didn't.

"No, it's fine. I'll take care of it." She didn't know how exactly. The only option she had was giving Madame Bonavich her drink which probably wouldn't sit well with the woman. She could only hope she was in a good mood.

"Again, I'm so sorry." The man ducked his head and scurried away looking like a scolded puppy with its tail between its legs.

Laney spared one glance at her formerly white shirt now stained brown and sighed. She was late; she didn't have the woman's coffee; and she looked like a slob. These were not the makings of a good day.

Continue reading The Cowboy's Reality Bride...

A FREE STORY FOR YOU

*E*njoyed this story? Not ready to quit reading yet?
If you sign up for my newsletter, you will receive
The Billionaire's Impromptu Bet right away as my thank
you gift for choosing to hang out with me.

The Billionaire's Impromptu Bet

A SWAT officer. A bored billionaire heiress. A bet that could change everything....

Read on for a taste of The Billionaire's Impromptu Bet....

THE BILLIONAIRE'S IMPROMPTU BET
PREVIEW

*B*rie Carter fell back spread eagle on her queen-sized canopy bed sending her blond hair fanning out behind her. With a large sigh, she uttered, "I'm bored."

"How can you be bored? You have like millions of dollars." Her friend, Ariel, plopped down in a seated position on the bed beside her and flicked her raven hair off her shoulder. "You want to go shopping? I hear Tiffany's is having a special right now."

Brie rolled her eyes. Shopping? Where was the excitement in that? With her three platinum cards, she could go shopping whenever she wanted. "No, I'm bored with shopping too. I have everything. I want to do something exciting. Something we don't normally do."

Brie enjoyed being rich. She loved the unlimited credit

cards at her disposal, the constant apparel of new clothes, and of course the penthouse apartment her father paid for, but lately, she longed for something more fulfilling.

Ariel's hazel eyes widened. "I know. There's a new bar down on Franklin Street. Why don't we go play a little game?"

Brie sat up, intrigued at the secrecy and the twinkle in Ariel's eyes. "What kind of game?"

"A betting game. You let me pick out any man in the place. Then you try to get him to propose to you."

Brie wrinkled her nose. "But I don't want to get married." She loved her freedom and didn't want to share her penthouse with anyone, especially some man.

"You don't marry him, silly. You just get him to propose."

Brie bit her lip as she thought. It had been awhile since her last relationship and having a man dote on her for a month might be interesting, but.... "I don't know. It doesn't seem very nice."

"How about I sweeten the pot? If you win, I'll set you up on a date with my brother."

Brie cocked her head. Was she serious? The only thing Brie couldn't seem to buy in the world was the affection of Ariel's very handsome, very wealthy, brother. He was a movie star, just the kind of person Brie could consider marrying in the future. She'd had a crush on him as long as she and Ariel had been friends, but he'd always seen her as just that, his little sister's friend. "I thought you didn't want me dating your brother."

"I don't." Ariel shrugged. "But he's between girlfriends right now, and I know you've wanted it for ages. If you win this bet, I'll set you up. I can't guarantee any more than one date though. The rest will be up to you."

Brie wasn't worried about that. Charm she possessed in abundance. She simply needed some alone time with him, and she was certain she'd be able to convince him they were meant to be together. "All right. You've got a deal."

Ariel smiled. "Perfect. Let's get you changed then and see who the lucky man will be.

A tiny tug pulled on Brie's heart that this still wasn't right, but she dismissed it. This was simply a means to an end, and he'd never have to know.

❀

*J*esse Calhoun relaxed as the rhythmic thudding of the speed bag reached his ears. Though he loved his job, it was stressful being the SWAT sniper. He hated having to take human lives and today had been especially rough. The team had been called out to a drug bust, and Jesse was forced to return fire at three hostiles. He didn't care that they fired at his team and himself first. Taking a life was always hard, and every one of them haunted his dreams.

"You gonna bust that one too?" His co-worker Brendan appeared by his side. Brendan was the opposite of Jesse in nearly every way. Where Jesse's hair was a dark copper, Brendan's was nearly black. Jesse sported paler skin and a dusting of freckles across his nose, but Brendan's skin was naturally dark and freckle free.

Jesse flashed a crooked grin, but kept his eyes on the small, swinging black bag. The speed bag was his way to release, but a few times he had started hitting while still too keyed up and he had ruptured the bag. Okay, five times, but who was counting really? Besides, it was a better way to calm his nerves than other things he could choose. Drinking, fights, gambling, women.

"Nah, I think this one will last a little longer." His shoulders began to burn, and he gave the bag another few punches for good measure before dropping his arms and letting it swing to a stop. "See? It lives to be hit at least another day." Every once in a while, Jesse missed training the way he used to. Before he joined the force, he had been an amateur boxer, on his way to being a pro, but a shoulder injury had delayed his training and forced him to consider something else. It had eventually healed, but by then he had lost his edge.

"Hey, why don't you come drink with us?" Brendan

clapped a hand on Jesse's shoulder as they headed into the locker room.

"You know I don't drink." Jesse often felt like the outsider of the team. While half of the six-man team was married, the other half found solace in empty bottles and meaningless relationships. Jesse understood that - their job was such that they never knew if they would come home night after night - but he still couldn't partake.

Brendan opened his locker and pulled out a clean shirt. He peeled off his current one and added deodorant before tugging on the new one. "You don't have to drink. Look, I won't drink either. Just come and hang out with us. You have no one waiting for you at home."

That wasn't entirely true. Jesse had Bugsy, his Boston Terrier, but he understood Brendan's point. Most days, Jesse went home, fed Bugsy, made dinner, and fell asleep watching TV on the couch. It wasn't much of a life. "All right, I'll go, but I'm not drinking."

Brendan's lips pulled back to reveal his perfectly white teeth. He bragged about them, but Jesse knew they were veneers. "That's the spirit. Hurry up and change. We don't want to leave the rest of the team waiting."

"Is everyone coming?" Jesse pulled out his shower necessities. Brendan might feel comfortable going out with just a new application of deodorant, but Jesse needed to wash more than just dirt and sweat off. He needed to wash the sound of the bullets and the sight of lifeless bodies from his mind.

"Yeah, Pat's wife is pregnant again and demanding some crazy food concoctions. Pat agreed to pick them up if she let him have an hour. Cam and Jared's wives are having a girls' night, so the whole gang can be together. It will be nice to hang out when we aren't worried about being shot at."

"Fine. Give me ten minutes. Unlike you, I like to clean up before I go out."

Brendan smirked. "I've never had any complaints. Besides, do you know how long it takes me to get my hair like this?"

Jesse shook his head as he walked into the shower, but he knew it was true. Brendan had rugged good looks and muscles to match. He rarely had a hard time finding a woman. Jesse on the other hand hadn't dated anyone in the last few months. It wasn't that he hadn't been looking, but he was quieter than his teammates. And he wasn't looking for right now. He was looking for forever. He just hadn't found it yet.

Click here to continue reading The Billionaire's Impromptu Bet.

THE STORY DOESN'T END!

You've met a few people and fallen in love....

I bet you're wondering how you can meet everyone else.

Star Lake Series:

When Love Returns: The first in the Star Lake series. Presley Hays and Brandon Scott were best friends in High School until Morgan entered their town and stole Brandon's heart. Devastated, Presley takes a scholarship to Le Cordon Bleu, but five years later, she is back in Star Lake after a tough breakup. Brandon thought he'd never return to Star Lake after Morgan left him and his daughter Joy, but when his father needs help, he returns home and finds more than he bargained for. Can Presley and Brandon forget past hurts or will their stubborn natures keep them apart forever?

Once Upon a Star: The second book in the Star Lake series. Audrey left Star Lake to pursue acting, but after an unplanned pregnancy her jobs and her money dwindled, leaving her no option except to return home and start over. Blake was the quintessential nerd in high school and was never able to tell Audrey how he felt. Now that he's gained confidence and some muscle, will he finally be able to reveal his feelings? Once Upon a Star will take you back to Christmas in Star Lake. Revisit your favorite characters and meet a few ones in this sweet Christmas read.

Love Conquers All: Lanie Perkins Hall never imagined being divorced at thirty. Nor did she imagine falling for an old friend, but when she runs into Azarius Jacobson, she can't deny the attraction. As they begin to spend more time together, Lanie struggles with the fact Azarius keeps his past a secret. What is he hiding? And will she ever be able to get him to open up? Azarius Jacobson has loved Lanie Perkins Hall from the moment he saw her, but issues from his past have left him guarded. Now that he has another chance with her, will he find the courage to share his life with her? Or will his emotional walls create a barrier that will leave him alone once more? Find out in this heartfelt, emotional third book (stand alone) in the Star Lake series.

The Heartbeats Series:

Where It All Began: Sandra Baker thought her life was on the right track until she ended up pregnant. Her boyfriend, not wanting the baby, pushes her to have an abortion. After the procedure, Sandra's life falls apart, and she turns to alcohol. Her relationship ends, and she struggles to find meaning in her life. When she meets Henry Dobbs, a strong Christian man, she begins to wonder if God would accept her. Will she tell Henry her darkest secret? And will she ever be able to forgive herself and find healing? Find out in this emotional love story.

The Power of Prayer: Callie Green thought she had her whole life planned out until her fiance left her at the altar. When her carefully laid plans crumble, she begins to make mistakes at work and engage in uncharacteristic activities. After a mistake nearly costs her her job, she cashes in her honeymoon tickets for some time away. There she meets JD, a charming Christian man who, even though she is not a believer, captures her interest. Before their relationship can deepen, Callie's ex-fiance shows back up in her life and she is forced to choose between Daniel and JD. Who will she choose and how will her choice affect the rest of her life? Find out in this touching novel.

When Hearts Collide: Amanda Adams has always been a Christian, but she's a novice at relationships. When she meets Caleb, her emotions get the best of her and she ignores the sign that something is amiss. Will she find out before it's too late? Jared Masterson is still healing from his girlfriend's strange rejection and disappearance when he meets Amanda. She captivates his heart, but can he save her from making the biggest mistake of her life? A must read for mothers and daughters. Though part of the series and the first of the college spin off series, it is a stand alone book and can be read separately.

A Past Forgiven: Jess Peterson has lived a life of abuse and lost her self worth, but when she is paired with a Christian roommate, she begins to wonder if there is a loving father looking down on her. Her decisions lead her one way, but when she ends up pregnant, she must make some major changes. Chad Michelson is healing from his own past and uses meaningless relationships to hide his pain, but when Jess becomes pregnant, he begins to wonder about the meaning of life. Can he step up and be there for Jess and the baby?

Sweet Billionaires Series:

The Billionaire's Secret: Maxwell Banks was the ultimate player until he found himself caring for a daughter he didn't know he had. Can he change to become the role model she needs? Alyssa Miller hasn't had the best luck with past relationships, so why is she falling for the one man who is sure to break her heart? Though nearly complete opposites, feelings develop, but can Max really change his philandering ways? Or will one mistake seal his fate forever?

A Brush with a Billionaire: Brent just wanted to finish his novel in peace, but when his car breaks down in Sweet Grove, he is forced to deal with a female mechanic and try to get along. Sam thought she had given up on city boys, but when Brent shows up in her shop, she finds herself fighting attraction. Will their stubborn natures keep them apart or can a small town festival bring them together?

The Billionaire's Christmas Miracle: Drew Devonshire is captivated by the woman he meets at a masquerade ball, but who is she? Gwen Rodgers is a teacher, but when she pretends to be her friend and meets Drew at a masquerade ball, her world gets thrown upside down.

The Billionaire's Cowboy Groom: Carrie Bliss finally found the man she wants to marry but there's just one little problem. She's technically still married. Cal Roper hasn't seen her in years but his heart still belongs to his wife. When she returns to town requesting a divorce, can he convince her they belong together?

The Cowboy Billionaire: Coming Soon!

The Lawkeeper Series:

Lawfully Matched: Kate Whidby doesn't want to impose on her newly married brother after their parents die, so she accepts a mail order bride offer in the paper. Little does she know the man she intends to marry has a dark past, sending her fleeing into a neighboring town and into Jesse Jenning's life. Jesse never wanted to be in law enforcement, but after a band of robbers kills his fiancee, he dons the badge and swears revenge. Will he find his fiancee's killer? And when Kate flies into his life, will he be able to put his painful past behind him in order to love again?

Lawfully Justified: William Cook turns to bounty hunting after losing his wife. When he suffers a life-threatening injury, he is forced to stay in town with an intriguing woman. Emma Stewart has moved back in with her widowed father, the town doctor, but she still longs for a family of her own, so no one is more surprised than she is when she starts to develop feeling for the bounty hunter, who hides his heart of gold behind a rugged exterior. Can Emma offer William a reason to stay? Can William find a way to heal from his broken past to start a future with Emma? Or will a haunting secret take away all the possibilities of this budding romance?

The Scarlet Wedding: William and Emma are planning their wedding, but an outbreak and a return from his past force them to change their plans. Is a happily ever after still in their future?

Lawfully Redeemed: Dani Higgins is a K9 cop looking to make a name for herself, but she finds herself at the mercy of a stranger after an accident. Calvin Phillips just wanted to help his brother, but somehow he ended up in the middle of a police investigation and caring for the woman trying to bring his brother in.

The Still Small Voice Series:

The Still Small Voice: Jordan Wright was searching for something after she gave her son up for adoption. What she found was God, and she began receiving visions. But can she trust Him when he asks her to do something big? Kat Jameson had long been a lukewarm Christian, but when her friend dies and she begins seeing lights, she thinks she is going crazy. Then she meets someone with a message for her. Will she be able to give up control and do what is asked of her?

A Spark in the Darkness coming soon!

Blushing Brides Series:

The Cowboy's Reality Bride: Tyler Hall just wanted to find love, but the women he dated wanted more than his small-town life provided. He gets more than he bargained for when he ends up on a reality dating show and falls for a woman who is not a contestant. Laney Swann has been running from her past for years, but it takes meeting a man on a reality dating show to make her see there's no need to run.

The Reality Bride's Baby: Laney wants nothing more than a baby, but when she starts feeling dizzy is it pregnancy or something more serious?

The Producer's Unlikely Bride: Justin Miller had given up on love, but when his image needs help, he finds himself needing the aid of a stranger who just happens to be a romance writer. Ava McDermott is waiting for the perfect love, but after agreeing to a fake relationship with Justin, she finds herself falling for real.

Ava's Blessing in Disguise: Five years after marriage, Ava faces a mysterious illness that threatens to ruin her career. Will she find out what it is?

The Soldier's Steadfast Bride: coming soon

The Men of Fire Beach

Fire Games: Cassidy returns home from Who Wants to Marry a Cowboy to find obsessive letters from a fan. The cop assigned to help her wants to get back to his case, but what she sees at a fire may just be the key he's looking for.

Lost Memories and New Beginnings: coming soon

Stand Alones:

Love Renewed: This books is part of the multi author second chance series. When fate reunites high school sweethearts separated by life's choices, can they find a second chance at love at a snowy lodge amid a little mystery?

Her children's early reader chapter book series:
    The Wishing Stone #1: Dangerous Dinosaur
    The Wishing Stone #2: Dragon Dilemma
    The Wishing Stone #3: Mesmerizing Mermaids
    The Wishing Stone #4: Pyramid Puzzle
    The Wishing Stone Inspirations 1: Mary's Miracle
    To see a list of all her books

authorloranahoopes.com
loranahoopes@gmail.com

ABOUT THE AUTHOR

Lorana Hoopes is an inspirational author originally from Texas but now living in the PNW with her husband and three children. When not writing, she can be seen kickboxing at the gym, singing, or acting on stage. One day, she hopes to retire from teaching and write full time.